THE SEARCH
Carol Fister Olvera

5624 Lincoln Drive Edina, Minnesota 55436

5624 Lincoln Drive Edina, Minnesota 55436

The Search

Copyright 1979 Jeremy Books. All rights reserved.

Library of Congress Catalog Card Number 79-84347
ISBN 0-89877-006-8

No part of this book may be reproduced in any form, except for the inclusion of brief quotations in a review, without permission in writing from the publisher.

Printed in the United States of America

FOR MOM AND DAD

... who know that for those who give their lives to God, all things work together in the best possible way to fit into His Masterplan ... and that if God—who gave up His own Son for them—is for them, then who or what can be against them, and who or what can separate them from His love?

—The Bible

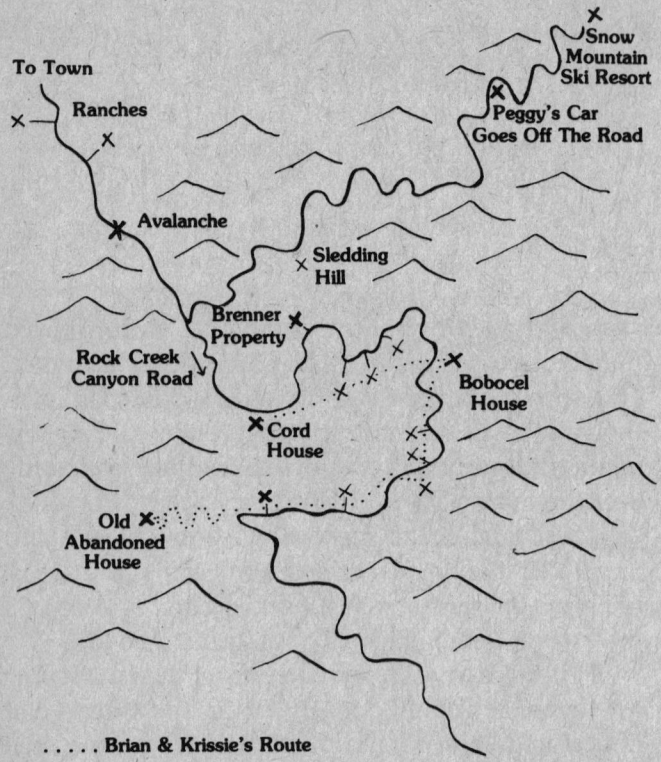

Part One

1

On a late November afternoon, a storm moved quietly across the Canadian border into Montana. The snow came gently at first, like a cold rain, wetting the earth but not sticking. Then, during the night, the ground freeze-dried, and the following morning a thin layer of white covered it. For three days and nights the snow sifted down steadily. It blanketed the weed clumps and lawns and trees, piled up on rooftops and parked cars, and coated the streets and highways and country roads.

Friday, a massive cloud cover began settling low over the mountains. By noon, the clouds had obliterated the mountains and there was no sky. Snow fell in thick, wet sheets. In town, the streets were slick with ice and slush, and five o'clock traffic was jamming up behind stalled cars and small accidents.

At his office near the edge of town, Jim Cord got up from his desk and stood at the window watching the snow. He was a lean, rangy man, in his late thirties, with strong hard hands that showed a lifetime of manual labor, and slightly graying sand-brown hair. His body was tense, his face gaunt and creased with a worry that had nothing to do with either the weather or the traffic. After a moment he returned to his desk. As he sat down, a feeling of incredible weariness settled over him, although he had done nothing physical all day. He ran the palm of his hand over his aching eyes, and then he picked a stack of bills off the desk and sorted through it. He added the amounts, wrote the total in pencil on the top envelope, wrapped a rubber band around the stack and dropped it in the bottom drawer with last month's unpaid bills. He was about to go over the accounts receivable page in his ledger, but instead he closed the book and locked it away in a fireproof safe in the corner. What was the use? No amount of figuring would change anything. Maybe he should throw in the towel, get out while he still could. But even as the thought of giving up stirred in his brain, a stubborn anger flared up inside him—an anger that would make him fight against the odds even if it killed him. He had never been a quitter. He wouldn't start now.

He got up and put on his coat and gloves and went outside through the shop, checking the doors and turning out the lights. His half-ton truck stood in the alley, frozen under a mound of snow. It occurred to him that he shouldn't have bought it last winter. But he had needed a new truck, and how was he to know his business would go sour? He opened the door and slid in, starting the engine and turning on the defroster. Then, while it was warming, he cleaned the snow off the windows and the hood.

As he drove out of town, Cord found himself thinking about his wife, Janet. He had kept his financial problems a secret from her, hoping for a break in this run of bad luck, but the situation had gone from bad to worse. He would have to tell her soon, but not yet. Not until he got it carefully laid out in his mind what he was going to do.

Nine years ago, when he told Jan he wanted to go into business for himself, she had cried. Her father had tried and he had gone bankrupt. It had destroyed her mother. She couldn't go through that again. But Cord went ahead, with Jan fighting him every inch of the way until she saw that he was a far better businessman than her father had been.

"What will she do when I tell her?" he wondered. For some idiotic reason he thought of the day he brought his first truck home and presented it to her so proudly, and she got the giggles and pointed at the magnetized rubber sign on the door and said: "Cord Electric! Electric cord! Get it?" The memory of it chafed on his ego the same as it had then, and hot anger boiled up inside him. It wasn't his fault. He had done his best, and it wasn't his fault.

His whole life was falling apart, piece by piece, and the thing he couldn't stand, the thing that made him crazy with anger and despair, was his utter helplessness to stop it.

Cord turned off the interstate at a large showy sign that read: SNOW MOUNTAIN SKI RESORT, and in smaller print underneath, Rock Creek Canyon. The wide dirt road had been graded and heavily sanded, and it wound lazily through the foothills past several cattle ranches for eight miles before it began its steep ascent into the mountains. Four miles beyond the last ranch, the road forked. Engraved in a small wooden sign was an arrow pointing to the left and the words "Snow Mtn Ski Resort—11½ m." Cord took the road to the right, to Rock Creek Canyon. Less than a quarter mile from the fork, he pulled into a long driveway that led to a beautiful cedar home.

The walks had not been shoveled since he had done them the night before. He stepped into the snow and took the wide, flat shovel from the side of the garage and dug it into the heavy crust of snow. Underneath, the walks were slick with ice. He hacked away at it with the edge of his shovel, a small irritation mounting within his mind. If Janet had kept after the walks today, they wouldn't be such a mess. He shoveled and hacked, shoveled and hacked. Before he had gone six feet, he was panting hard and sweating. His neck under his collar was wet, and the sweat was rolling down his chest and his back and it soaked through his t-shirt and his flannel shirt to his coat. He stopped and leaned on the shovel.

The front door opened and Janet stuck her head out. "What are you doing?"

"What does it look like!"

"It's suppertime. The roast is drying out."

"Let it dry out then! Since I'm the only one around here who can shovel the walks I guess I'll keep going until I've finished them."

"What do you think I do all day? Sit around and watch soap operas or something? I've hardly had a chance to sit down and eat, much less to worry about the stupid walks!" Janet went back inside, closing the door loudly, to show him she was mad.

Cord bent down and continued shoveling the snow. He felt lousy about biting her head off like that. He even halfway enjoyed cleaning the walks. He wanted to say he was sorry, not just for tonight but for all the silly spats he had caused during the past few months, but he knew that he wouldn't. He knew that as soon as he walked into the house his apology would stick in his throat, and that if he tried to say anything he'd end up making things worse.

When he had finished the walks, he leaned the shovel against the garage, stamped the snow off his boots and went into the house. He was hot and thirsty and aching with tiredness.

"Hi Daddy." His six-year-old daughter held out her arms for a hug.

"Hi Krissie." He leaned down and kissed her. "Where's Michael?"

"He's sick," Krissie answered.

Cord looked at his wife. "What's wrong?"

"I don't know. Another nasty cold, I suppose. His throat hurts. He's a little feverish."

"Did you call the doctor?"

"No, I didn't call the doctor. He just started getting sick a few hours ago." She filled a plate and set it in front of him. "Everything's cold now."

He shrugged. She could have kept a plate in the oven for him, the way she did when she wasn't mad. Well, he didn't care one way or the other tonight. He wasn't particularly hungry.

The phone rang. "I'll get it!" Brian and Krissie jumped up from the table and raced for the phone.

"I said I'd answer it!" Brian said, shoving his younger sister back.

"You always get to answer the phone! Mom!"

Cord got up and went into the living room. "I'll answer it." He lifted the receiver. "Hello?"

"Hi Mr. Cord, is Brian home?"

"It's Richie, Brian. Keep it short."

Brian took the phone. "See. It was for me anyhow."

"You just think you're so smart because you're eight and I'm only six," Krissie said. "Well, someday..."

"Knock it off, both of you!" Cord went back to the kitchen. He was getting a headache. As he ate, he could feel Jan watching him with her quiet brown eyes that saw everything. He wondered how much she had guessed already.

Janet got up and started clearing the table. "Do you want anything else?"

He shook his head.

She opened her mouth to say something, then changed her mind, turning away from him to the sink.

"Guess what?" Brian came into the kitchen.

No one answered him.

"Richie Brenner got a snowmobile of his very own! His dad wanted everybody in the family to have his own because it's more fun that way. Boy, we don't even have one."

"We can't afford one," Cord said.

"Richie said we could get a secondhand one like his. They don't cost so much. Could we, Dad? Could we get just one snowmobile?"

"No."

Brian's shoulders sagged. "Richie's so lucky. His dad gets him everything."

Cord felt black, bitter anger roar through his brain. He flung his arm out and brought the back of his hand across his son's cheek. Brian sprawled onto the floor, more from surprise than from the blow. Krissie started sobbing.

Cord walked into the living room and turned on the TV, hating himself for what he was doing to his family. He heard Jan tell the kids to play quietly in their rooms until bedtime.

It was late when he finally went to bed. Janet lay with her body turned stiffly toward the wall. He eased himself onto the bed beside her and closed his eyes. But he didn't sleep. In the middle of the night, he heard Michael cry out. Janet slid soundlessly from the bed and went to him. Nearly an hour passed, then he heard water running in the bathroom sink, and a little later, Jan came back into their room.

"Is he worse?" Cord asked.

"He's just all stuffed up. I rocked him back to sleep."

"Did you put the vaporizor in his room?"

"Yes, Jim, I put the vaporizor in his room."

"I was only asking, that's all."

She didn't answer, and when he reached out and touched her, she didn't respond.

Tomorrow I'll tell her, he thought. Tomorrow I'll tell her everything.

2

At 5:30 a.m. Cord got out of bed, dressed in the dark and went into the bathroom. He turned on the cold water faucet, bent down, cupped his hands and splashed the icy liquid over his face again and again until it numbed the massive ache in his head. He rinsed the cottony taste from his mouth and took two aspirins. Then he went into the kitchen and made a pot of coffee.

Why me, God? Why my business? He sat down heavily, dropping his head into his hands, the question echoing through his brain. He had a deep, genuine faith in God that came up from his childhood, and he had never questioned the logic of that faith until the past few months, as his business had gone downhill. Now he found himself questioning it more and more frequently. He hated the feeling of uncertainty it dredged up inside him. He had always been so sure before—sure of God, of himself, of his direction in life.

He did not hear his wife come into the kitchen. She stood quietly in the doorway, watching him, reading the despair and discouragement in his body. It was tearing her apart to see him this way, to lie awake at night and feel him twist and turn on the bed beside her. Knowing that something was eating away at him and not knowing what that something was filled her with dread. Why was it so hard for him to share his problems with her? Why couldn't he admit to her that he couldn't always handle everything alone, that sometimes he failed, that sometimes he needed her? Or was it that? Maybe . . . She shook away the ugly fear that had been skirting the edge of her mind lately, and suddenly the thought of going through another day of this was more than she could stand.

"Jim?"

He started. "What are you doing up so early?"

"I could ask the same about you." She poured a cup of coffee and sat down, probing his face with her eyes. "We have to talk."

He felt a small jab of anger at her invasion of his privacy. He wasn't ready yet. He needed more time to set it up in his brain, to find the best words.

"You can't keep shutting me out!" she cried. "I have to know what's bothering you! No matter how bad it is, it couldn't be any worse than anything I've already imagined." Her voice broke, and Cord knew without looking at her that her eyes were filling with tears.

Please don't cry, he pleaded silently. I can't deal

with your tears now. "I didn't want to worry you," he said aloud. "I wanted to work it out. I didn't want you to know."

Jan shoved back her chair and went to the sink, wiping up the coffee grounds he had spilled. Her stomach was tight with fear. "Is it . . . is it another woman?" she asked finally. Her hands trembled.

Cord stared at his wife incredulously. "Of all the crazy things!" If she hadn't looked so pathetic he would have laughed. "As long as I live I'll never understand a woman," he said. "My business is falling apart and my wife thinks . . ." He shook his head slowly. "And I thought you knew me so well." He got up from the table and went to her, turning her around to face him. "You know I love you."

"I haven't been so sure lately."

"I'm sorry. I know I've put you and the kids through hell. It's just that everything I've worked so hard for is slipping away from me."

"You should have told me. You should have let me help."

"There was nothing you could do."

"It would have helped just to share it with someone. That's what a wife is for. To share the bad times, not just the good times." She poured more coffee and sat down, waiting.

Cord looked out the window at the thick swirl of white snow falling in the early morning darkness. If it kept up this way, they'd have a real mess on their hands. Thank goodness there was a ski resort up the road. Otherwise they'd be snowbound most of the winter. Not that it would be a bad idea right now. At least if they were snowbound he could avoid that stack of unpaid bills.

He sighed deeply, remembering Jan, and sat down across the table from her. Where should he begin? And how would he tell her they might have to sell the place?

Jan reached out and took his hands in hers. "I've never seen you like this before. It must be pretty bad. Are we going bankrupt?"

"Not if I can help it."

"Then what? I want to know everything, Jim. How long has the business been going downhill?"

"Since last winter, I guess. There wasn't enough work to keep my men busy. Then I lost a couple thousand dollars when one of my customers went bankrupt. And people weren't paying their bills."

"That's happened before."

"Yeah, to a certain extent it has. But not like this. It's always picked up during the summer. This summer it didn't. We lost some regular customers when I raised my prices. Then we wired those five houses for Jennings Construction and he skipped town without paying his bills."

"But you said you had liens against the property."

"I did, but they aren't worth much."

"Why?"

"It's too complicated to go into right now, Jan," he said wearily.

"You won't get any of your money?"

"Not much."

"That was thousands of dollars!"

"Yes."

She was silent, her mind working feverishly for some solution. "Can't you get a loan from the bank until you get back on your feet?"

"The bank won't loan me any more."

"What are we going to do?"

"I don't know," he said, "except sell this place."

"No! There has to be something else."

"Do you think I haven't gone over every possibility? I don't want to sell any more than you do. I even considered selling the business. The banker says sell the house."

"I can get a job."

He shook his head.

"That's stupid! The only reason you won't let me is because of your dumb male ego."

"Jan, if I thought for one minute that having you work for awhile would solve everything, I'd gladly let you do it. But we need the money now, not in six months, and we need a whole lot more than you could earn in six months anyhow."

"I don't want to sell the house!"

"So what do you want me to do? Sell the business? Try to find a regular job? Is that it?"-

"Maybe it wouldn't be such a bad idea. All you care about is that stupid business."

"It's that stupid business that got you the house in the first place!"

The phone rang. "I'll get it," Cord said. As he

strode angrily into the living room he nearly knocked Brian off his feet. "What are you doing up so early?"

"I—couldn't sleep."

Cord picked up the receiver. "Hello."

"Jim Cord?"

"Yeah."

"This is Bill Moore. I own the last ranch before the Rock Creek Canyon turn-off."

"Yeah, I know the place."

"I know it's early and it's Saturday and it's a lousy time to call, but our electric heat isn't working and we're half-frozen."

"I'll be right there."

"We'd sure appreciate it."

"I'll be charging double time."

"That's fine. We just want some heat."

Cord hung up the phone and got his coat.

"Where are you going?" Jan asked.

"I have a service call."

"I was hoping you'd have some time for the kids today."

"You're the one who's upset because we don't have the money to keep our house and now you're griping because I get a little work?"

"A service call isn't going to make any difference."

"Every job helps," he said coldly.

"Unless I'm the one working. Right?"

"Knock it off, Jan."

"No, I won't knock it off. I'm angry."

Cord opened the door and stepped outside, glad for the chance to be getting away for awhile. He wished he could be gone all day.

It was cold, but not too cold, and the sky was pregnant with more snow. The trees sagged under the weight of yesterday's snow, and already some of their branches had buckled and ripped off. The electrical wires overhead were sagging too, stretched almost to their limit.

Cord scooped up a handful of snow, shaped it into a ball and sent it thudding into the side of his pickup.

Brian watched his father drive away from the house. He felt awful inside—sick and worried and scared—after what he'd heard.

He hadn't meant to stand in the hall, listening to his parents. He'd come right to the kitchen door before he'd started listening to their words, and once he'd heard what they were saying, he'd ducked back into the hall and listened to the whole thing.

He didn't understand everything his dad had told his mom, but he understood enough to know that his dad needed a lot of money and that they were going to sell their house and everything to get it. He didn't want to live somewhere else. He'd always lived here across the field from Richie Brenner. If they moved, he'd probably never see his best buddy ever again. He'd hate that.

But that wasn't the worst part. The worst part

was thinking of how his mom and dad were always yelling at each other lately. There were some kids at school whose moms and dads were always mad at each other, and after awhile they didn't want to live together anymore.

Brian blinked his eyes fast to keep the tears from spilling out all over his face. He couldn't let on to his mom or to anybody that he'd heard them talking. They'd be pretty mad if they found out.

He went into the living room and stretched out on the carpet beside Krissie, but he couldn't get very interested in the cartoons. He kept thinking about last night when dad had hit him on account of the snowmobile. Last night he had felt like running away and never coming back, and all he had thought about was how mean his dad was getting.

But now he knew why his dad was so grouchy all the time. He remembered a few months ago when he begged and begged for a ten-speed bike, and how when his dad had said no, he had said all kinds of mean things about how he liked Richie's dad better and how he wished he could live over there.

He hadn't meant all that stuff. He really hadn't. If he had known that his dad didn't have any money, he wouldn't have asked for anything. He wished he could throw his arms around his dad's neck and tell him he was sorry. He wished he could tell him it didn't matter a hoot about the bike and the snowmobile or anything else either. But he couldn't, of course, because then his dad would know that he'd been listening.

"Brunch is ready," his mom called from the kitchen.

Brunch on Saturday mornings was always Brian's favorite meal of the whole week, unless his mom made fried chicken or something like that. But today he didn't feel like eating anything. He wasn't very hungry.

"Brian!"

"Dad's not here," he mumbled.

"He can eat when he gets back."

Brian could tell by the way her voice sounded that she was still mad at his dad, and that made him feel even worse.

"What's the matter with you?" his mother asked.

"Nothing." He knew he'd better eat or she'd ask a bunch more questions and he didn't want that. So he jabbed his fork into the stack of French toast, poured syrup all over it, scraped some bacon onto his plate and shoved some into his mouth. There was a big lump stuck in his throat from not crying when he needed to, and he nearly gagged, but his mom was watching, so he kept swallowing until the lump and the food went all the way down.

"You and Krissie can go outside and play after you eat," his mom said.

"Me too," Michael said.

"No, not you. I'm keeping you inside today."

Michael started crying, and Brian didn't hear his dad come into the house.

"What's wrong with him?" he asked.

"He wants to play outside," Krissie answered.

"Why can't he play outside?"

"Because he had a fever last night," Brian's mom said.

"Cut it out, Michael," his dad said.

Michael quieted down and so did everyone else.

"How about if we build a snow fort this afternoon," his dad said finally. "The snow is perfect."

"Really Daddy?" Krissie said. "You too?"

"Me too."

"Oh boy!" Krissie jumped down from her chair. "Come on Brian. Hurry up and finish eating."

Brian stared miserably at his plate. He wished they would all go away and leave him alone. The phone rang and his dad went to answer it.

"Brian . . ."

He glanced up at his mom. Now what?

"Are you still mad at Daddy because of last night?"

He shook his head.

"Are you sure? Honey, Daddy's going through a very bad time right now. He has some big problems and he doesn't know what to do about them. I know he's been grouchy lately, but we have to try to help him by not saying and doing things that upset him more. Don't be mad at him. Try to understand."

"You're mad at him!" he accused.

"Brian!"

"Well, you are!" He couldn't stand another minute of this. He was going to cry and he didn't want them to see him. He shoved back his chair and raced off to his room. He buried his face in his bed and sobbed and sobbed until he was exhausted. Then he sat up and rubbed at his eyes with his fists and blew his nose hard. He'd be okay now.

But he had to get his dad some money...

He breathed a hole in the frost on the window and looked out. His dad was leaving again. That meant he must have another job. If only he could get a job. If only he were older. There were a thousand things a guy could do if he were older. But he was only eight. What could a little kid do to get money?

"Brian!" His mom knocked on the door, but she didn't come in the way she usually did.

"What?"

"What are you doing?"

"Nothing."

"Dad wants you to shovel the walks for him before the snow piles up on them again."

"Okay." He waited until he heard her walk away, then he slipped out of his room, put on his jacket and mittens and went outside before she could see from his face that he had been crying. His dog came whipping out of his doghouse and jumped all over him.

"Get down, Zane. I don't feel like playing today." He found the shovel and worked at the walks, all the while trying to figure things out.

He had nearly finished when suddenly he knew how he could help. It wouldn't get him a lot of money, but his dad had said that every little bit helped!

His thoughts raced. He wouldn't tell anyone. Mom probably wouldn't let him do it, and anyhow, he couldn't tell her without explaining why he wanted the money and then she'd know he was out there listening this morning. He'd do it secretly. He could get lots of walks to shovel as long as it kept on snowing, and he'd hide the money in his room, in a place his mom would never see it, and he'd save it until he had a whole bunch. Then he'd take it out and hand it over to his dad.

But how was he going to do it without them finding out? What could he tell his mom so she wouldn't know or guess? How about if he took his sled along and said he was going over to play with Richie? Yeah. That might work. He always went over there anyhow.

Brian was so excited he dropped the shovel and hurried into the house. He pulled on his long underwear, an extra pair of socks, his boots and a ski cap.

"Where are you going?" Krissie asked.

"Someplace that's none of your business."

"You're going over to Richie Brenner's, aren't you? You're going to the sledding hill. I want to go too."

"No way."

"Mom said you have to take me this time."

"The snow's too deep for you. You wouldn't have fun."

"I want to go."

"You don't need to go. You spoil everything."

"I'll tell Mom. Mom!" Krissie yelled.

"What are you two fighting about now?"

"Brian's going to Richie's house to go sledding and I want to go. You said I could, Mom. You said I could go the next time he went."

"You promised you'd take her, Brian. Remember?"

"Aw, Mom. She ruins everything. Nobody else has to take a little sister everywhere."

"That's enough, Brian. If you don't want to take her, you can just stay home."

Brian glared at his sister. Now what was he going to do?

"I better not hear that you've been mean to her either," his mom threatened. "Understand?"

Krissie smiled triumphantly as she pulled on her snowsuit.

Brian sat on the floor and stared at his feet. What should he do? Forget about going? But he had to go. The snow was too good to pass up today. And what if it didn't snow any more for awhile?

Maybe he should tell Krissie what he was really going to do. She was a pretty okay little kid about keeping secrets and all. Then if he told her, she wouldn't want to come.

"Krissie," he whispered.

"What?"

"Can you keep a secret?"

"What kind of a secret?" she asked suspiciously.

"You have to promise not to tell anybody. Especially not Mom and Dad. Cross your heart and hope to die?"

"Okay. Cross my heart and hope to die."

He glanced at his mother in the other room and leaned over closer to his sister. "I'm not going to Richie's."

"Where are you going then?"

"I'm going to a whole bunch of houses and I'm going to shovel the walks."

"Why?"

"So I can get some money."

"You're just saying that so I won't go. I'll tell Mom."

Brian clamped his hand over her mouth before she could yell again. "I'm telling the truth. Scout's honor. I'm going to give the money to Dad after I get enough."

"Dad doesn't need any money."

"Yes he does. He needs a *lot* of money. I heard him and Mom talking in the kitchen this morning. We might have to move away from this house and everything."

Krissie's eyes widened at the thought of it.

"Dad and Mom are really worried about not having money. And Mom is sad about having to leave the house."

"I saw her crying today."

"See? That's why I have to help them. But it has to be a secret."

"I want to help too."

"You can't shovel snow. It's too hard for you."

"Well, what can I do then?" She got her face all wrinkled up like she always did when she was going to cry.

"Don't cry! Then Mom will ask what's wrong."

"I want to give Dad some money too. I can help with my little shovel. I help Dad. He lets me clean the edges so it looks nice and straight."

"It'll be awfully hard work."

"I don't care."

Brian sighed. "Okay. You can help. But you better not cry and stuff when you get tired."

"I won't."

Brian went into the living room where his mom was rocking Michael. "We're leaving."

"Okay. No fighting now."

"We won't."

"And don't stay too long. Remember, it gets dark early now."

"I know, Mom." He turned to leave.

"Oh, and by the way, Dad said you kids should stay away from those big cottonwood and maple trees along the road. The snow is so heavy and wet that great big branches are cracking and breaking off."

"We'll take the short cut across the field," Brian said.

The two children went outside. "You get on the toboggan," Brian told his sister. "You can carry the shovel and I'll pull you. It'll be faster that way because the snow's pretty deep for you."

Krissie sat down and took the shovels obediently. "How will I hold on?"

"I won't go fast." Brian took the rope and plodded through the snow along the fence that marked the edge of Brenner's property, beyond it to the houses higher up in the canyon.

3

Brian was discouraged. Nothing was going the way it was supposed to. Nothing at all. They had been out here at least an hour and they hadn't gotten one single job yet.

For one thing, it was taking forever to pull Krissie through so much deep snow. He wished he had never let her come along. And then, when they finally got to the first two houses, the walks were already clean. And at the third place no one was home. Now at this house, the man who answered the door said he'd get his own kid to do it later.

Brian plodded on up the canyon. His legs were getting awfully tired and Zane kept running in front of him and making him trip.

"I don't think we'll ever get some money for Daddy," Krissie said, sighing loudly.

"Yes we will," he said stubbornly. "I've been praying and praying. I know God will get us a job."

"He might not. Mommy said that sometimes God doesn't answer our prayers because He doesn't think we should get what we asked Him for."

"Well, He's gonna answer this prayer!" Brian answered angrily. "He knows Daddy really needs the money."

"Maybe He's mad because we lied to Mom."

He hadn't thought of that. What if God was mad at him for lying? He had an idea. "I lied, but you didn't. Why don't you pray?"

"What should I say?"

"Just ask Him to get some jobs for us."

Krissie squeezed her eyes shut tightly and worked her mouth silently. "Maybe I better say it out loud just in case He didn't hear it."

Brian nodded. He was sure God had heard, but all the same . . .

"Dear Jesus," Krissie prayed, "please help us get some jobs shoveling sidewalks so we can get some money for Dad. Jesus' name amen."

Brian hauled the sled over a small rise in the ground. Ahead of them was a house with a huge yard. All around the yard there was a high chain-link fence and on top of the fence there were three strands of barbed wire. Plastered all over the place were big red warning signs that said: BEWARE OF DOGS. Zane stiffened and growled deep in his throat.

It was Chuck Bobocel's place. His heart sank all the way down to his toes. He could never go in there. Not in a million years! Chuck Bobocel raised the biggest, meanest dogs he had ever seen, and they could tear a kid like him to pieces in one minute flat. Once, when he and Richie Brenner were going up the road to go fishing, two of the dogs had come close to breaking the fence down trying to get at them. Both of the boys had been scared to death.

Brian stopped, grabbing hold of Zane's collar. What should he do? Richie Brenner had told him once that Bobocels were almost as rich as his dad. They would probably pay them pretty well, and the walks weren't done yet.

"What's the matter?" Krissie asked.

"I'm thinking." He couldn't see any dogs. Maybe they were locked up in their kennels. He could rattle the gate just to see. He turned to his sister. "You stay here. Hold onto Zane as hard as you can. Don't let him get away for anything." He put Krissie's hand on the collar. "Sit!" he ordered the dog. "Stay!"

"What are you doing this for?"

"Because there's a whole bunch of mean dogs in there and I have to check first and make sure they're not out in the yard."

Krissie's eyes got big and scared-looking. "I want to go home. I don't like this place."

"They can't get out of the yard."

"What if they jump over the fence?"

"They can't. Now just be quiet and hang onto Zane." Brian approached the fence cautiously. His heart was thumping and pounding and knocking around inside him so hard he could hardly breathe. Everything was dead silent. He reached out and jiggled the gate loudly.

The hounds came streaking around the house from the back. Brian's heart jumped a mile. Krissie screamed. Zane jerked away from her and tore across the snow.

In the yard, the dogs threw themselves against the fence in a frenzy of hatred, barking and growling and showing their teeth. On the outside, Zane was just as mad and mean. Brian stood there, half-paralyzed with fright. Behind him, on the sled, Krissie sobbed hysterically.

A woman came out of the house to see what the racket was all about. "Hey!" she yelled. The dogs didn't even pay any attention. Then she took a whistle from her pocket and blew on it. The dogs dropped away from the fence.

"Get back there!" she told them. "Go on! Go to your kennels!"

The dogs slunk away from the fence with their tails between their legs. Even Zane stopped barking and hung his head.

The woman came across the yard to the gate. "Did you want something?" she asked.

Brian nodded. "Are you Mrs. Bobocel?"

"I sure am." She smiled. "What's your name?"

"Brian Cord."

"Is that your little sister?"

He nodded. "Her name's Krissie." He turned and waved at her to come.

Krissie was still worried about the dogs. She came reluctantly, keeping her eyes on the back of the house, all tensed up in case they came roaring around again.

Mrs. Bobocel saw the fear in her face. "It's okay, honey," she said kindly. "They won't bother you again. Actually, they're very nice dogs. They just get excited and mad when strangers come around."

Brian didn't believe that part about how nice they were, but he didn't think he should say anything. She might get mad and then she wouldn't let them shovel her walks. Although—he looked past her to where the dogs had disappeared—he didn't know if he wanted to go in there or not, even if she stayed out with them.

Krissie walked back to the sled and sat down. She wasn't going in that place, no matter what.

"You wanted to see me?" Mrs. Bobocel asked.

"We want to know if we can shovel your walks."

"Oh. Well, I really don't need anyone to do that for me. When my husband gets home, he'll clean them off with the snow blower. It only takes him a few minutes and it's very easy to do." She smiled at them. "Do you live around here? I haven't seen you before."

"Our house is the first one in the canyon."

"The one that has all those beautiful flowers around it every summer?"

"Yep. That's the one," he said proudly. "My mom always plants them there." Then he remembered that she wouldn't be able to do that anymore because they were going to sell the house. He blinked hard to keep from crying. Nothing was working out the way it was supposed to.

"You're kinda far from home. I bet you're cold and hungry. How about if I make you a nice snack. Some cookies and hot chocolate?"

Brian shook his head. "We have to go. We have to find some walks to shovel so we can earn some money. Only nobody will hire us."

"You must be planning to buy something very special."

He shook his head. "No. It's for ... it's for ... " He decided it would be okay to tell her. She didn't know his mom and dad anyhow. "It's for our dad," he told her. "He needs some money real bad and he's going to sell our house and Mom is sad and they're always mad at each other and worried and grouchy."

Mrs. Bobocel was deeply touched. "That's the sweetest thing I've ever heard. You know something? I've been thinking. It's snowing again and by the time my husband gets home, he'll be mighty tired and he won't feel like cleaning the walks. And the snow will be so deep by then that it'll clog up the snow blower. I bet he'd be really glad if someone helped with the walks."

Brian's face lit up eagerly. "Do you think so?"

She smiled. "I'm sure of it!"

Brian's face broke into a wide grin. He swiped at his eyes. "That'd be super!"

"By the way, how much do you charge?"

He hadn't thought about that. He thought people would know how much to pay them. "I don't know."

"Well, I'll see what kind of job you do, then I'll decide how much. Is that a deal?"

He stuck his hand out. "It's a deal. Hey Krissie! We got a job! Did you hear that? Come on! Let's get working!" He went running to the sled for the shovel.

"I'm not going in there," Krissie stated. "I don't like those dogs. I want to go home."

"You promised to be good, Krissie."

"I'll lock the dogs up in the kennels," offered Mrs. Bobocel.

"Come on, Krissie. We've got a lot of work to do."

Krissie hung back.

Brian grabbed her by the arm and dragged her along with him.

"I'll go right now and lock up the dogs so they can't get out," Mrs. Bobocel said gently. "Okay?"

Krissie nodded.

The woman opened the gate and both children drew back.

"We'll wait," Brian said.

She smiled at them. "I'll be back in a minute."

Much later, Brian was sure his arms were going to fall off. He had never shoveled so much snow in all his life. He looked back and saw his sister far behind him, scraping the edges carefully.

"Hurry up!" he shouted.

"I'm hurrying as fast as I can!"

"Well, you have to try harder, that's all. If we don't hurry up and finish we won't have time to do any more sidewalks today." He went back and helped her.

"I'm too tired to do any more walks."

"I told you it was too hard for you, but you had to come, and now you're stuck here until I'm ready to go home. I'm tireder than you are. I had to pull you all the way here."

They were almost to the front of the house when Mrs. Bobocel came out to inspect their job. Brian crossed his fingers hopefully. She just had to pay them well.

"This is a wonderful job!" she exclaimed. "Now why don't you two come inside and rest a bit. I'll get that snack I mentioned earlier and you can dry out by the fire."

"We should be going," Brian said.

"You'll be able to work better if you take a break," she said. "You must be about ready to drop after all that work."

"Well, I guess we could rest," Brian said. "But only for a minute." He wished she would tell them how much she was going to pay them, but she didn't say anything. A dreadful thought occurred to him. What if she was only going to give them a snack instead of money? He had to know. He cleared his throat nervously. "Have you decided how much you're going to pay us?" he asked in a small voice.

Mrs. Bobocel smiled. "I sure have. I was going to give you ten dollars, but you did such a lovely job I've decided to give you fifteen instead. How does that sound?"

Brian gasped. Fifteen dollars! He could hardly believe it! He followed Mrs. Bobocel into the house. "Fifteen dollars!" he whispered to Krissie. "Wow!"

The woman handed him two crisp bills. "I'll give the money to your brother," she told Krissie, "but half of it is yours. Is that all right?"

Krissie nodded.

"Thanks a million!" Brian nearly shouted. He could have hugged her.

Mrs. Bobocel took their wet clothing and laid it out in front of the fireplace to dry. Then she had the children sit down and warm themselves while she poured them some steaming hot chocolate and set a big platter of cookies in front of them.

It felt good to sit down. The fire made them feel warm and sleepy. They didn't want to leave, but Brian knew they had to be getting on if they were going to get some more jobs. But before they left, there was something he had to ask Mrs. Bobocel. He had sort of gotten the idea when he was outside shoveling snow, and now that he had that money folded up in his shirt pocket, he knew it was a good idea, provided, of course, that she agreed.

"Mrs. Bobocel," he asked, getting up. "Do you

think you'll need someone to shovel the walk a little some other day?"

"Well . . . I don't know. I'll have to talk to Mr. Bobocel."

"Please? Oh please make him say yes!"

"I'll see what I can do."

"And I was wondering if I could do some jobs around here in the summer too."

She laughed. "You certainly are ambitious!"

"My dad needs all the help he can get."

"Well your dad sure is lucky to have a boy like you. I'll talk to my husband tonight and we'll see what we can come up with."

"I'll call you," Brian said. "This is a secret." He nudged Krissie, who was nearly asleep. "We have to go now."

Krissie sighed, climbed out of the chair and started pulling on her snowsuit.

Mrs. Bobocel dumped the rest of the cookies into a plastic bag. "Take these along. You might get hungry."

"Thanks, Mrs. Bobocel," they said, going outside.

"Don't go too far up the canyon," she called after them. "It's getting late."

"We won't."

At the bend in the road they turned and waved. Then they hurried on to the next house.

"Let's go home," Krissie begged. "We already have lots of money."

"It's not enough. We couldn't even buy a bike

with fifteen dollars. Dad needs hundreds of dollars."

"Well, we can't get that much!"

"I know, but we have to get more than this."

Krissie's shoulders slumped. "But I'm too tired to work some more."

"Just quit it. I knew you weren't tough enough to help."

"Well I didn't think we'd have to work all day!"

"It isn't all day."

The people at the next two houses didn't want them to shovel walks for them, but at the third, some nice old people said they would pay them five dollars to clear a path from the door to the driveway.

"You should be getting home," the man told them as he handed them their money. "Where do you live?"

"Down the canyon."

"Want me to give you a ride?"

Brian shook his head. "There are still a couple more houses that aren't too far away."

"Well don't be too long, son. There's a storm brewing."

"We can take a short cut straight from the last house to our house. Our house is really close if you don't go all the way around the loop on the road."

"Just don't get lost."

"We won't. Richie Brenner and I take the short cut all the time during the summer when we go fishing in the creek."

It was snowing when Brian and Krissie came to the last house, and a nasty wind had started to blow in small, chilly gusts. Brian looked up at the darkening sky. That storm was coming. Maybe they should just get home.

He touched his pocket. They had made twenty-five dollars. That was enough for one day, wasn't it? He was getting really tired now. Besides, the way the snow was starting to blow around nobody else would want walks cleared because it wouldn't do any good.

"Let's go home," he said.

4

At home, Janet Cord had spent most of the afternoon entertaining Michael. At noon she had given him another aspirin, which had brought his temperature down to normal, but had left him feeling much too well to sleep and not quite well enough to play nicely on his own.

They gathered up all his blocks and dumped them in a heap in the middle of the floor. Then they constructed a miniature town. They drove little toy cars and trucks through the streets. They crowded plastic animals into the tiny zoo. They moved gumdrop-shaped wooden people from the houses to the stores to the zoo and back to the houses.

Janet's mind wasn't really on their game. She kept going over and over what Jim had told her earlier that morning. The enormity of it all had her completely floored.

If only he had told her sooner, she kept thinking. If only he hadn't waited until the whole mess was so far out of hand! If only he had come to her in the beginning! She could have gone to work then, even part-time. But no, his ridiculous male ego forced him to do everything alone. It made her mad! Look at what his pride was going to cost them now.

She looked around at the house. All her life she had dreamed of a place like this. A beautiful home with a fireplace and lots of kitchen cupboards and a garden and a yard full of trees and flowers.

Janet's eyes filled with angry tears. It wasn't fair! She had never lived in anything but a trailer until Jim had bought this place, and the thought of going back to one was more than she could bear. She didn't want to work, no matter what she had said to Jim, but she would a whole lot rather work than lose the house.

Stupid people who refused to pay their bills! How she hated those who cheated and stole from others! Jim had struggled for years to build up his business, and now, because of a few miserable thieves, he might lose everything. Why did God let things like this happen to those who belonged to Him? Why had he let Jim get involved in a contract that would ruin him?

She remembered how he had worried over the shortage of work last summer. It had had something to do with several small electrical contractors in town whose prices were low because they hired apprentices instead of journeymen, Jim had told her, and he could have fought them but he preferred not to. He had believed God would work things out.

Then Jennings Construction had offered him a big contract, and it had seemed to be the answer to his prayers.

No wonder he had become increasingly bitter toward God. Not that he ever said so, but she could sense it in him. It was as if God had put a rug underneath him and told him to stand up, and then yanked the rug away.

On the other hand, maybe Jim had jumped without really praying about the job. And yet, why hadn't God stopped him somehow from making such a costly mistake?

Her mind was cluttered with confusion and anger. *I need You,* she prayed silently. *I don't want to doubt You this way.*

Michael tugged insistently at her sleeve. "Mommy!"

She brought her attention back to him. "What?"

"I want to hear my Three Little Pigs record."

She got up and put the record on for him. Halfway through the story he didn't want to hear it anymore. She sighed and turned it off.

"I want to color now."

"Oh Michael!" She always hated this stage of the kids' sicknesses. They could be so pesky. She found his coloring book and a box of crayons, and sat at the table with him. He scribbled on a few pictures, then closed the book.

"I'm hungry, Mommy."

"What are you hungry for?" she asked. He had hardly eaten a thing since yesterday.

"I'm just hungry."

"How about an egg?"

"No."

"A cheese sandwich?"

He shook his head.

She decided to simply go ahead and prepare something for him since he didn't know what he wanted. He would eat if he was hungry. She went to the kitchen and quickly prepared some orange juice, toast, and instant bouillon.

Michael nibbled at the toast, refusing to even so much as taste the soup. He drank all the juice. Then he put his head down on the table.

"Don't you feel good?"

He shook his head. "I want you to hold me."

Janet looked at him closely. His face was flushed and his eyes listless. Instinctively, she reached down and touched the back of her hand to his forehead and his cheeks. His hot skin burned against hers.

She found the thermometer and took his temperature. It was 102. She fed him another orange-flavored children's aspirin and bathed his face and hands with cool water.

"Does your throat hurt?"

He shook his head.

"Does your tummy hurt?"

"Nothing hurts," he said irritably.

She wondered if she should call the doctor. Well, maybe she should just let him sleep awhile. His nose was stuffed up. It was probably only a nasty cold.

"I want you to read Peter Rabbit to me, Mommy."

Janet carried Michael to the swivel rocker, sat down with him and started to read. Within minutes he was sleeping. She continued to rock him gently, knowing that if she moved he would awaken.

She wondered when Jim would be finished at Snow Mountain Ski Resort. Probably not until late. What had he said wasn't working? The T-bar? That always took awhile to repair. Well, at least they would pay well. Sometimes, though, she wished he could stay home and they could forget about money.

She was beginning to feel more and more terrible about the ugly way she had exploded at him this morning. When he so desperately needed her love and understanding, she had only added to his problems. No wonder he never wanted to share with her.

They used to share everything. Even the business. In those first few years he had used the garage as his shop and the spare bedroom as his office. It had been a tiny room, barely able to contain the old desk and filing cabinets. He couldn't afford to hire a secretary, and he didn't really need one then anyhow, so she had answered the phone and kept the books.

It hadn't been easy. She had hated the constant phone calls, the customers banging on the door, the crew clumping through the trailer with their buddy boots, and the noisy CB radio with its static and unknown voices. And after Brian was born and they had to cram his crib into their small bedroom it got even worse. During the days his feedings and naps were constantly interrupted. During the nights he was too tense and tired to sleep well and so he kept her and Jim awake.

But they had survived. They had worked together. They had shared and been happy, and they had built a good business. In spite of all the bad times it had been wonderful those first years. She had been so much a part of her husband then.

Funny how the bad times hadn't seemed so bad then. Maybe it was because they had had so little to lose. Now it was killing them to have to struggle— to think of giving up what they had. They could give up half of what they had today and still have more than they had in those days.

The thought made her ashamed.

What was it she had read yesterday morning in her Bible? Something about how God expected His people to be content with whatever they had, that they should be grateful for it no matter how small it was, and that they should never worry about things, because God would always give them what they really needed and that was all that mattered.

Yesterday the familiar words hadn't meant much to her. Now she knew they were exactly what she needed.

It was always that way between her and God. She was reading straight through her Bible, from beginning to end. Every morning she read one chapter or less, depending on the length of it, and every morning it was as if God had just finished writing it because the words she read were so right for the day. Sometimes she didn't realize how important they would be to her until later, but always they were what she needed.

How could anyone doubt the reality of God? How could people not believe that the Bible was a living letter from a personal God?

"Thank You for being here whenever I need You," she whispered.

Michael shifted in Janet's arms, trying to turn onto his stomach. She eased herself slowly, carefully, from the rocker, swaying her body slightly to continue the rocking motion after she was standing. She walked across the room and laid him on the sofa.

He awakened immediately and began to cry.

Janet lifted him up again and returned to the chair. She reached behind her and pulled an afghan off the back of the chair and draped it over them both.

She rocked quietly. Michael closed his eyes and slept again. The house was warm and silent and beautiful.

"I still can't give it up," she said out loud. Her eyes filled with tears. Then she leaned her head back and slept too.

At Snow Mountain Ski Resort the storm had already struck. Jim Cord waited impatiently in the control shack at the bottom of the T-bar for Arnie to pick him up in the snowpacker and take him below to the chair lift. It had taken him all afternoon to get the T-bar running smoothly and the skiers who had swarmed all over the slopes earlier were gone.

He glanced at his watch. Four thirty-five. By the time he got home Jan would be furious. He had let the kids down again. Sometimes he wondered if it was worth it. Maybe he should sell his business and settle into some regular eight-to-five job.

He felt his bitterness and anger toward God expanding and growing like a malignant tumor in his chest. There was supposed to be a reason for everything that God allowed to happen in the lives of His people, but what possible reason could He have in this? It was nothing but a waste. A waste of time and effort and money. What possible good could come from such a mess? It certainly wasn't helping his family.

His mind returned to his wife. He had expected her to go to pieces over the failing business but she had taken it rather calmly. He wondered if he would ever really know her.

But then, dummy that he was, he had to go mention selling the house on top of everything else he had bombarded her with. He should have waited until she had recovered from the rest. If he had waited she might have come to that conclusion herself.

Cord wiped a clear spot in the tiny window of the shack with his sleeve and peered out into the darkness. "Come on, Arnie!" He had a sudden urgent need to get home to his family.

5

Brian was all mixed up.

No matter which way he turned, everything looked the same. He couldn't tell which was front and which was back.

He had been in these trees a thousand times and he had never gotten mixed up before. He and Richie Brenner always cut through the trees when they went fishing in the creek on the other side of the road past Chuck Bobocel's house because it was a lot faster that way. But it looked all different now. There weren't any paths and the trees made spooky shadows and weird noises when they rubbed together.

He wished that he hadn't come this way. He should have stayed on the road. Then he could have sat on the toboggan with Krissie and they could have slid part of the way. And he could have walked in the tire tracks from the cars instead of all this deep snow. He wouldn't have been confused on the road either.

But when they had left that last house on the road there was a loud cracking sound that had scared the wits right out of him! He had whipped around just in time to see the whole top of one of those huge cottonwood trees come crashing down smack dab in the middle of the road.

Then he remembered what his mom had said about staying away from those trees, and when he thought about how they grew all along the road he decided to take the shortcut for sure. Besides, he had been certain he could get home a lot faster. How was he supposed to know he'd get lost?

It hadn't been too bad at first. The snow was deep—right up to his knees in some places—but he was doing okay. When he got tired, he found a place in the bushes where the wind couldn't get them and they pretended it was their house and they were eating supper.

Krissie pulled the bag of cookies from her pocket. They were mostly squashed and broken, but the children didn't care. They laid the best ones out on top of the toboggan and let Zane have the crumbs.

"Let's pretend we're having fried chicken tonight," Krissie said. "This is the chicken and this is, umm, this can be the dessert. It's chocolate cake."

Brian groaned. "Don't remind me of all that good stuff."

Krissie sprinkled snow on the cookies. "That's ice cream on top." She gave Brian two cookies.

"Here's your supper. We don't have to eat any vegetables because we're grownups and nobody can boss us." She hated vegetables. Every night at supper she gagged before she got them all swallowed.

They ate their cookies. Then Krissie brushed the crumbs off the toboggan and wiped her hands on her snowsuit.

"That was very delicious," Brian said, trying to sound like his dad. "You're a good cook."

She kissed his cheek. "Thank you."

"Yuck!" He jumped up and wiped it off. "How come you did that?" he asked, glaring at her.

"Mommy kisses Daddy."

"Well, we're just playing and you don't have to kiss me. I hate getting kissed."

"Even when Mom kisses you?"

"Sometimes. Like if she kisses me when Richie is there."

"Oh."

"We better get going," Brian said.

"Well, let's play like we're pioneers," she suggested. "Like on TV. The toboggan can be our covered wagon."

"Okay. I guess I'll have to be the horse."

"We could let Zane be the horse and you could be the driver. I bet he'd make a good horse. He could probably go faster than you."

"Zane isn't big enough."

"He is too."

"He is not. I bet he couldn't even pull you." He

looped the rope around his stomach and waited for her to climb onto the toboggan. "I'll be the horse. Zane can just be our dog."

After that it kept getting worse and worse. Brian's legs were so tired they didn't want to move any more. He leaned his body forward, letting the rope kind of hold him up, and dragged the toboggan. Every couple of steps it got stuck and he had to yank hard to get it going again.

The wind kept slapping the snow into his eyes and nose and mouth, and it kept trying to rip his hood right off his head. He had to put his head down low or he couldn't even breathe. He turned around and walked backwards. He could see Krissie on the toboggan, all hunched over with her head on her knees. She was hanging onto the shovels with one hand and onto the sled with the other. She kept trying to lift her head, but the wind would knock her breath away and she'd have to lower it again. He couldn't tell if she was crying or not but he figured she was.

He didn't know what to do. He didn't know which way to go and he kept bumping into trees. It was getting darker and darker every minute.

He was so cold and tired. He was hungry too, or maybe he was just feeling scared way down in his stomach. He stopped and put his arms up in front of his face to keep the snow away so he could see where they were. But he was too mixed up, that was all there was to it. He dropped his arms hopelessly.

Zane came to him and licked his wet mitten,

whining softly. Brian patted him. Then suddenly he knelt down and hugged his dog tightly, burying his freezing face in Zane's neck. The dog's short hair was all wet and cold and smelly. "I bet you could get us home, couldn't you, boy."

Zane whined and lifted a paw.

Brian stood up and pointed. "Home," he said. "Find the way home, Zane."

The dog barked and ran forward.

Brian started yelling joyously. He ran, stumbling and floundering through the drifts after the dog. The toboggan jerked, dumping Krissie, and the lightened load sent Brian sprawling headlong into the snow. Krissie sat on the ground, wailing and digging at her eyes with her wet mittens. Brian went back and helped her up and brushed her off.

"Don't cry," he soothed. "Pioneers never cry."

"Well, you dumped me off the toboggan."

"I didn't mean to! Besides, I fell right on my face and I'm not crying."

"I want Mommy!"

He patted her. "I'm sorry I made you fall, Krissie. I was trying to catch up to Zane. He's going to help us find the way home."

Krissie stopped crying. "Are we lost?"

"Just a little bit."

"Well I don't like it here! I want to go home."

"Then get back on the sled so we can get home," he ordered.

"I'm tired of these old dumb shovels," she said, sniffing loudly.

"We can't leave them here. Dad would get really mad." He wondered if his dad had come home yet. What if he had tried to shovel the walks and couldn't find the shovel?

He slipped the rope over his head again and turned to see if Krissie was ready. She was. He strained forward, following Zane through the trees.

But he couldn't keep up. His legs kept folding under. He was so tired. And thirsty too. He scooped up a handful of snow and stuck it into his mouth, remembering how his dad had told him once that you were supposed to hold it in your mouth and warm it up before you swallowed it or it would make your insides cold and pretty soon it would make you cold all over. The snow felt good on his dry tongue. He let it stay there until finally it seeped down his throat.

He struggled to his feet and started walking again. He walked and stumbled and fell and got up again, and it seemed like forever. He was getting really scared now. It was almost completely dark and he couldn't see anything.

He hated it when it was dark outside and he was in the woods, even when he was hanging onto Dad's hand. He wished he was at home. He clenched his teeth and balled up his fists to keep from sobbing aloud. He couldn't cry now or he might not be able to stop. And that would get Krissie going too.

Brian stopped dead still. Something huge and black was crouching in the snow in front of him. He let the rope slide from his waist and stood there, frozen with horror, fused to the ground, staring at the thing.

Krissie moved up beside him and found his hand in the darkness. "What is it?" she whispered.

"I don't know."

The wind roared through the trees, and something like an enormous clutching hand reached up from the Thing. Brian scrambled madly to get away, but the Thing grabbed at his legs and he smacked into the ground. A sob tore at his throat. He closed his eyes and waited in utter terror.

"Brian! Brain!" Krissie was screaming and yanking at him.

He rolled over and felt the rope twist around his legs. He sat up carefully, keeping his eyes glued down at the ground, and pulled the rope off him. He stood up. And then he made himself look up at that place where the Thing had been.

It was still there. It hadn't moved closer at all. Brian reached down and wrapped his hand around Zane's collar. With his other hand, he hung onto Krissie. Mustering all the courage he possessed, he took a small step forward.

Nothing happened. He took another step. Then another and yet another.

Suddenly he understood. It was that weird-shaped tree that he and Richie Brenner liked to climb! He ran forward and leaned against it, limp all over with relief.

Now he knew where they were! They were close to the old abandoned house where he and Richie had their super secret hideout.

Man, it was the best hideout in the world, too. They had found it one day when they were playing that they were detectives in search of clues in a haunted house. There was a small trap door in the kitchen floor, and down below there was a root cellar. They took a solemn oath never to tell anyone about their hideout as long as they lived, and then they even scratched their wrists with a pin and held them together and became blood brothers.

Richie had smuggled all kinds of things into the hole. He brought a raggedy old tarp from his dad's garage and they spread it out on the floor. One time he brought two old fruit cake tins filled with candles and matches and candy. They kept all their secret maps and codes in another tin box. They used tin boxes because Richie said the mice would chew up cardboard boxes.

He stopped thinking about the hideout and wiggled his toes around. The cold was seeping into him and he was shivering. They would have to get home soon or he wouldn't be able to make it.

Then it hit him that they were still terribly far from home. They had already gone past the house, way behind it, and now they were as far away from home as they had been when they had first taken the shortcut. Only it was a whole lot worse now because there weren't any houses nearby where they could get help.

What were they going to do? He couldn't walk that far, and besides, he didn't even know which direction was which.

"Brian!" Krissie tugged at his arm. "Let's go home."

She was going to start crying again, he could tell, and he didn't think he could stand that. But how could they ever get home now?

Maybe they should stay in the hideout! Just until it got light enough to see.

But there was the oath he had made with Richie.

"Brian!"

He made up his mind. They would never be able to make it home tonight. It was too dark and he was so tired he could hardly pull the toboggan or even walk. And the snow was getting deeper and deeper.

Richie would understand about the hideout. They were blood brothers and that meant that if one of them was going to die the other one would do anything he could do to keep him alive. So Richie would think it was okay for him to take Krissie to the hideout. And he would make Krissie promise never to tell anyone.

Once he had made up his mind, he moved quickly. He made his way straight ahead, in the direction the crooked tree was pointing. The old house loomed up in front of them.

"Whose house is this?" Krissie asked.

"Nobody's. Come on. Let's go in."

"I don't want to! I want to go home!"

"Well, we can't. It's too far and we can't see in the dark. Do you want to get lost again?"

"No."

"Well, then we have to stay here."

"I want to go home! I want Mommy and Daddy."

"Be quiet!" he shouted. "In the morning we'll go home, when we can see." He grabbed her hand and dragged her behind him through the door.

"It's freezing cold in here," Krissie wailed. "It's dark. I'm scared. I don't like this place."

Brian groped through the darkness, stumbling over parts of the ceiling that had caved in to the floor, and found the kitchen.

"Brian!" Krissie howled. "Don't leave me here alone! I can't see!"

He went back and took her hand. "Well, come on then!"

"We'll freeze to pieces in here."

"We will not." He found the trap door. A heavy beam from the ceiling lay over it. He heaved and shoved. "Help me move this," he grunted.

Krissie knelt down beside him and together they worked the beam away from the door. Brian found the rusty old ring and lifted the door carefully.

"Don't move around or you'll fall in," he warned.

"What is it?" she asked, frightened.

"A cellar, kinda. We can stay down there."

"I don't want to go down there!"

"It'll be warmer down there than up here with the wind blowing on us. Now just be quiet." He felt around for the ladder and climbed down carefully.

"Brian!"

"I'm right down here. I'll try to find a candle and some matches." He ran his hand over the shelves until he found one of the round tin boxes. He tried to pry it open but his fingers were cold and clumsy. He removed his mittens and used his fingernails. The lid came off suddenly and everything spilled onto the floor. He groped around on the tarp for the matches.

"Hurry up," Krissie said above him.

"I'm trying. Quit bugging me." His fingers closed around a little glass cup with a short, fat candle in it. Then he found a book of matches. He tore one out, felt for the scratchy stuff on the box and scraped the match against it several times. It flared up, blinding him. He burned his fingers and dropped the match. It went out. He lit another one, and another and another. Each time, the match went out before he could light the candle. Finally there were no more matches.

He tried to find another book on the ground, but there didn't seem to be any more.

"You'll have to come down in the dark," he said.

"I can't." Krissie started crying again.

"I'll help you," he said wearily. "It's not very far down." He climbed up the ladder and reached for her. "Turn around and put one leg down and I'll put it on the ladder for you."

"I can't!"

"You can too! If you don't come down here

you'll have to stay up there alone and freeze to death."

Krissie turned around carefully and eased her leg toward the edge. Brian grabbed it and pulled her closer. Krissie screamed. "I'll fall!"

"No you won't. Now let me put your foot on the ladder. I'll be right behind you so you won't be able to fall. Okay?"

Krissie lowered her leg over the edge and let her brother place her foot on the ladder. She clung tightly to the top until she felt both feet firmly in place on the rung. Slowly and with desperate care she climbed down into the cellar.

"Come on, Zane," Brian coaxed.

The dog barked and whined and circled the opening several times, but refused to jump.

"Okay then, stay up there." Brian climbed up and pulled the trap door down, jamming a hunk of wood in it so it wouldn't close all the way. Zane whimpered and Brian patted his nose. "You should have jumped down, boy," he said.

He climbed back down, and the two children curled up against each other and pulled the tarp around them. Within minutes, they were snoring softly.

Above them, Zane whined and sniffed at the trap door. Then he lay down.

Outside, the storm raged.

At home, Janet awakened abruptly. The house was dark and cold, and she could hear the wind rattling against the walls outside. A thin line of fear crept in around the edges of her brain. Where were the kids? And where was Jim?

Michael stirred restlessly in her arms, seeking the heat of her body. "I'm cold," he complained.

She wrapped him in the afghan and got up.

"Is it nighttime?"

"I guess it is." She wondered what time it was. She reached out to turn on the lamp. It didn't go on. Stupid bulbs! They always burned out at the worst times! She crossed the room and tried another one. It didn't go on either.

So the electricity was off. She had better dig out the candles. No wonder the house was so cold. Thank goodness they had a fireplace!

But first she had to call Brenners to make sure the kids were okay. She felt her way into the kitchen and found a flashlight in one of the drawers. The small yellow beam of light poked into the darkness. Janet shined it on her watch. It was 6:15.

"Mommy!" Michael cried. "I'm scared in the dark by myself! How come you don't turn the lights on?"

"Because I can't. The lights don't work." She went in to him.

"Can I hold the flashlight?"

"Okay, but you can't play with it. You'll have to shine it where I tell you."

"I will, Mommy."

She picked him up and gave him the flashlight. They went to the phone and Janet picked up the receiver. The phone was dead. She should have known the phones would be dead if the power was out. Or did they have anything to do with each other? Did you need electricity to make a phone work? Oh for Pete's sake! What a ridiculous thing to think about at a time like this. What difference did it make?

What should she do? Get the car out of the garage and drive over to Brenners'? She hated to take Michael out into the cold, but she could bundle him up. She wondered if the car would even start. Well, she had to get the kids.

She dressed Michael quickly and wrapped him in the afghan again, then pulled on her own coat and boots.

"Where are we going?"

"To get Brian and Krissie from Brenners'." She opened the door. The wind tore it from her grasp and slammed it inward against the wall. The snow was a thick white swirling mass descending on them. Janet pushed the door shut with her body and leaned against it, trembling. She couldn't go out there! She was scared to death of driving on snow anyhow. What was she going to do?

"Get hold of yourself," she said. "Don't panic."

"What, Mommy?"

"I was just talking to myself." She carried Michael into the living room and sat down, trying to think. It wasn't all that late, really. There was nothing to worry about. Aggie Brenner was one of those over-protective mothers when it came to her youngest son, Richie. Well, she wasn't that bad actually, but she did keep a close eye on him. Janet was pretty sure that the minute it looked like it was going to storm Aggie had hurried outside to get the kids in. That was one reason she never minded letting Brian and Krissie go all the way over there by themselves. She knew that Aggie would take good care of them.

Sid must be gone or Aggie would have had him drive the kids home. She would never do it herself, of course, because she was even worse about driving on icy roads than Janet was.

The only thing Janet couldn't figure out was why Aggie hadn't called her to let her know the kids were okay. Unless the phones had been out-of-order for quite awhile. That was certainly possible. Then, too, the kids might have told her they didn't have to be home until dark.

"Why aren't we going?" Michael asked.

"It's too nasty to drive. Daddy will be home soon and then he can get them." But where was Jim? What if he had gone off the road somewhere? Worry and fear tightened her throat. Sometimes she hated living way out here!

She took off their outdoor clothes, then rummaged around in the bedroom for some candles.

Michael shone the flashlight into her eyes. "I'm cold, Mommy."

She wrapped one of her sweaters around him. "I'll build a nice fire in a minute." She found the candles, took them into the living room and lit them. The soft glow melted the darkness away. Then she made a fire.

Janet leaned back in the chair with Michael against her and listened to the storm. There was no point in getting all knotted up with worry.

And yet . . . The fear still lurked in the corners of her mind.

Where were they?

Part Two

6

Peggy Caldwell had awakened that morning at 6:00 as usual, even though she was on vacation and didn't have to go to work. No matter how hard she tried to sleep and no matter how tired she was, she always woke up at six.

She sat up in the bed and looked around, trying to decipher the unfamiliar room in the darkness. Where was she?

Then she remembered. She had come to Snow Mountain Ski Resort because she needed to get away for awhile. As she reached out to turn on the lamp beside the bed, her arm brushed against something, knocking it to the floor. She switched on the lamp and saw that it was her 8 x 10 gold-framed wedding picture. She picked it up and stared into Tom's smiling face. It didn't look like him. None of the pictures she had looked like him. They were nothing more than flat pieces of paper that didn't move or feel or smell or taste or touch or laugh, with faces that had been frozen into eternal lifeless smiles. The way he had been when he was dead.

Oh Tom ... The familiar emptiness filled her soul until her body ached with it. She set the picture back on the nightstand and got up.

As she opened her suitcase she found a Bible on top of her clothing. Her mother must have slipped it there just before she left yesterday evening, hoping against hope that she would read it.

Peggy flipped through the familiar pages to the book of Psalms. But it was no use. The words meant nothing to her. Between her and God there was a wall—the wall of her doubt in Him, the wall of her bitterness and of her guilt. No matter how badly she wanted to be able to break down that wall, she couldn't. God had taken Tom away from her. He had smashed her dreams. It was something she couldn't understand, and because she couldn't understand, she couldn't accept it. She couldn't trust God again. She tried, and once in awhile she thought she was going to be okay, but always, in a day or so, all the doubt and depression came flooding back, crowding out the feeling of peace and leaving her even emptier than before.

She laid the Bible aside and dressed slowly in jeans and a red and white ski sweater. She brushed out her long, dark hair, remembering how Tom had liked her to wear it loose and free around her face, saying it made her eyes even bluer. Now she wore it up or pulled to the back of her neck with a rubber band. There was no man she wanted to impress or please.

Several days before, her mother had commented on how she never fixed herself up anymore the way she had when Tom was alive. "I wish you'd go out and find yourself a nice young man and get married again," she had said. "Then I wouldn't have to be always worrying about you."

"Nobody said you had to worry. I make out okay."

"You're not making out okay at all, Peggy. You've got to forget about Tom. He's dead and nothing will bring him back to you. You need to get out and meet other young people and have fun. Most of all you need a husband."

"I don't want another husband."

"Then think about little Roddie! He needs a father!"

"Yes," Peggy had said bitterly, "he needs a father. And he had a good father until God took him away."

"I can't understand what's been happening to you lately," her mother had said. "You took it so well in the beginning. You keep to yourself too much. You have too much time to think."

"The only reason I made it at first was that I was in shock, Mother. That's all. I couldn't feel anything. Now the shock is finally wearing off. I hurt. Is that so bad?"

"It is if you let it destroy your life."

"God destroyed my life, not me."

"Oh Peggy, please don't be like this."

"I can't help it, Mother. I wish Roddie and I could have died with Tom."

"What an awful thing to say."

Peggy stared at the bitterness etched across her face in the mirror. It had been an awful thing to say, but she had meant it. Why not be dead? She had no reason to live now.

She pushed the thought abruptly from her mind, turning away from the mirror. What should she do now? It was still too early for skiing. She turned on the TV. Cartoons. Suddenly she missed her year-and-a-half-old son. On the Saturdays she had off, he always came into her bedroom and hauled her out of bed. Then she made a special breakfast and they sat together in the living room and ate on TV trays and watched cartoons. In the afternoons they always went to a drive-in for hamburgers and milkshakes, then to the park or bike-riding. That was one of the highlights of her life.

It could have been so wonderful. If it hadn't been for the death of her husband, Peggy would have been a missionary nurse in Bolivia.

It had been her childhood dream.

Her father was a pastor and she had grown up surrounded by missionaries who stayed in their ample five-bedroom house while they presented their work to the people in the congregation. She had listened wide-eyed and eager to their adventures and watched their slides and heard them appeal to others to care enough about those who had nothing to give up their comfortable lives and to help them. She had hardly been able to wait until she was finished with high school so she could start making her dream come true.

Then, after high school, she decided to become a nurse so she could help them physically as well as spiritually. She believed strongly that the physical, the emotional and the spiritual parts of a human being were closely bound together and that each one deeply affected the others. So she spent three years in nurses' training and another two in a Bible college.

It was there that she met Tom Caldwell, a big husky guy with a friendly grin and a hearty laugh and a love so great for his God that he could actually make other people love Him just by talking about Him. And Tom had a dream too. He was an agronomist and he was going to Bolivia as soon as he finished his missionary training.

It was as if God had planned for them to be together from the beginning. Falling in love was the natural thing for them to do. And they did.

They were married the day after Tom's graduation. A year later, Peggy finished her second year. She also gave birth to a son. In three months they had their passports, their shots and the money they needed to get to Bolivia.

Before they left, they drove West to say goodbye to her parents and to let them see their grandson, as well as to present their work to the people in her father's church.

It was early April, and in Montana, it was snowing. The highways were slick and dangerous.

Tom said, "Maybe we should stop at a motel for the night. It's getting pretty bad."

She shook her head. "We'll be home in a few hours. Besides, we can't afford a motel. Do you want me to drive? Are you getting too tired?"

"It's not so much that I'm tired," he said, "as it is that I'm worried about the driving conditions."

"I wouldn't mind driving. I'm used to this kind of stuff, you know. Why don't you let me drive as soon as I finish feeding Roddie?"

"I suppose it'd be all right," he said reluctantly, "but I still think we should stop. There's a town not too many miles ahead. We could both use some rest."

"Let's just get home," she said. She fed and changed the baby, then gave him to Tom, taking his place behind the wheel. An hour passed. Peggy found herself getting sleepier and sleepier, and the visibility worse.

And then, out of the snowy darkness came a truck. It loomed in front of them for one hideous fraction of a second. Peggy screamed.

All night, she stood in the waiting room at the hospital. She had forgotten her baby. She was unaware of her parents and the friends who had come to be with her. She stood at the window watching the snow. Tom had wanted to stop and she wouldn't let him. It was all her fault. She should have stopped. But she had said no, and now . . .

She wanted to go in to him, to be with him. She could hear him in the emergency room, crying out in pain, pleading with them to help him. But they shut her out.

In the morning, it became quiet. They came and told her he was dead.

Just like that. Gone forever.

And God had killed him.

Peggy hadn't thought of it in quite that way until recently. When she talked to people who asked about her husband, she always used neat little cliches like: "God took him home" or "He passed away about a year ago." She could never say something like "God killed him." But she could think it and know it to be true in her heart.

And wasn't it the truth? Didn't God control the universe? Didn't He have the ultimate power over life and death? She could cover it up with all the nice words in the world, but it didn't change the ugly facts.

Why? Why had He taken the life of a man like Tom Caldwell, whose greatest desire was to make other people know and love Him?

And what about her? What about all the things she was going to do for Him? God had not only destroyed one life, but two. And for what?

Never once had it ever occurred to Peggy that her dream of becoming a missionary might be unfulfilled. Everything had been so right until the night Tom died.

Even a month after the funeral, she had decided to go ahead with her plans. It was the one thing that kept her from falling apart.

And then the mission board told her she couldn't go. It would be different, they said, if she had already spent a few years in Bolivia. Or if she didn't have a baby to care for. But along with her adjustment to widowhood there would be the added pressure of new motherhood and of adjusting to a new culture and way of life. She would have no friends or family to lean on. There would be no one to help her with her child. She would have to learn a new language . . . No, they said, they didn't think it would be wise for her to go now. Maybe in a few years.

She had never made any alternative plan for her life. Now it lay shattered at her feet and she had nothing to live for.

She had moved back home with her parents and gotten a job at the hospital. Her life was neither good nor bad. She simply existed from one day to the next. After several months had passed she found an apartment and moved into it so she and her son could have a life of their own.

Her mother had objected strongly. "Why can't you stay with us? We have more than enough room. You shouldn't be alone."

"I'm not your little girl anymore, Mom," she had said gently. "Besides, we're not that far away."

She said nothing about how she wanted to be alone, whether she should be or not.

And now the aloneness, the boredom, the eternal emptiness was consuming her. The gray fog of depression was closing in on her, pressing down on her, crushing her. She was on the verge of a nervous breakdown and she could feel herself spinning like a top into it.

That was why she was here, at Snow Mountain Ski Resort.

Peggy turned off the TV and went out to the cafeteria. She ordered a bowl of peaches and some coffee. She ate slowly, waiting with the few other early risers for daylight.

Outside, the snow was falling in thick feathery flakes. Peggy took a deep breath, gulping at the coldness in her throat and nostrils. She stuffed her hair under a blue stocking cap and caught a chair on the lift. Slowly she swung out over the world.

She had forgotten how beautiful it was on the slopes and how invigorating the air felt. It had been a long time since she had been skiing. Until she met Tom she had wondered how she would ever live without it. As she skied the slopes and the hours raced by, she wondered if her parents had been right about this being the best therapy in the world for her.

It was midafternoon before she finally called it quits. Her whole body throbbed with aching muscles and sheer exhaustion, and she was incredibly hungry. She unstrapped her skiis and went inside the lodge. When she had finished eating a chicken dinner with apple pie a la mode, she went to her room and stretched out on the bed. Within minutes she was sleeping.

Her dream began with a void. Then, very slowly a soft light began to glow, dispelling the darkness. Peggy looked around. She stood in the middle of a path that wound steadily upward to an incredibly beautiful place filled with flowers and trees. It was a place of sunshine and laughter, and Tom was there, smiling at her and waiting for her to come. Then someone whose face she couldn't see came to her and beckoned her to follow him.

She began to climb, rapidly at first, then more and more slowly as the path became steeper and more difficult, and the way seemed unending. As time passed, the light began to dim until she couldn't see where she was going. She stumbled and fell.

"Help me!" she cried in terror.

Then, out of the darkness, a hand appeared, and the voice of the one whose face she couldn't see said: "Follow me."

Peggy struggled to her feet and followed the hand, groping and scratching and clawing desperately at the side of the mountain. Just when she thought she could go no further, the hand reached out and took hers.

"One more step," the voice said.

She surged ahead joyously, and suddenly, she was falling, falling, falling into an abyss. The one whose face she couldn't see laughed.

"I trusted you!" she cried. "I trusted you!" The darkness closed around her.

Peggy bolted upright in the bed with a sob. Her body was wet with sweat and her brain, thick with sleep, refused to function. The room was dark and cold. She shivered and reached out to turn on the light. It didn't work. In a panic she ran to the door and flung it open. The hallway was dark, but she could hear talking and laughter in the lounge. She groped her way toward it.

The lounge was aglow with candlelight. Skiers sat or stood around the fireplaces. Peggy read her watch: 5:30.

"Is the power out?" she asked a young man.

"Yeah. It went out awhile ago."

"What happened?"

"There's a bad storm outside. Where've you been?"

"Sleeping," she said. She looked around at the groups of skiers. She didn't want to be alone in that cold, dark room. She found a chair and sank into it.

"Mind if I join you?"

It was the man she had been questioning. She smiled and shook her head.

"Can I get you a drink or anything?"

"No."

"In that case I'll sit down." He took the chair next to her. "Are you here alone?" His eyes went to her left hand.

"Yes."

"That's good to know. I noticed you this morning in the cafeteria. Caught a glimpse of you once or twice on the slopes too. You're good. Do you ski often?"

"I used to until I got married."

"I didn't think..."

"I'm a widow," she said tightly.

"I'm sorry. I didn't mean to put my nose where it doesn't belong. Although I'll have to admit that I have been wondering if an attractive woman like you could still be single."

Peggy felt herself getting tense. Why did there always have to be some stupid guy around trying to hustle her? Why couldn't men see that she wasn't interested? She should have remembered to wear her wedding ring.

"By the way, my name's Gregg Johnston. Yours?"

"Peggy Caldwell."

"Glad to meet you, Peggy." He grinned, and something about his face reminded her of Tom.

She stood up quickly. "Excuse me," she whispered. "I'm awfully tired."

He stood up and took her elbow. "Can I help you to your room?" he asked with concern. "You look terrible."

"No. Please. I'll be okay. I just need to lie down." She tried to smile politely. "I think I overdid it today." She hurried back to her room and lay on the bed and cried. She should have known that coming here wouldn't change anything. If only she were dead. There would be peace. . .

Like someone in a trance she went to her suitcase and felt around in the side pockets for her bottle of sleeping pills. She opened it and dumped the pills into the palm of her hand. It would be so easy to die.

Suddenly cold, clammy terror clamped itself onto her brain. Her thoughts became frantic, scrambling, incoherent. What was she doing?

"I have to get out of here," she said aloud. "I have to go home!"

She packed her suitcase and found her way through the darkness to the office. It was empty. Well, never mind. She could call tomorrow and let them know she had checked out. Maybe they would return her money and maybe not. It didn't matter.

She hurried outside to the parking lot. Thank goodness she had been lucky enough to get a spot near the door. She might never have found her car otherwise.

She was just leaving when a jeep pulled up beside her and honked at her to stop. She rolled down her window and a deputy sheriff stuck his head out of the jeep.

"Are you going back to town?" he asked.

"Yes."

"The road is getting bad. You might want to stay overnight and try it in the morning."

She shook her head. "I have to get back tonight. I've driven in this kind of weather before."

"Okay," he said, "but be careful. That road out there isn't the same as the freeway or the streets in town."

"Thanks," she said. "I'll be careful." She rolled up her window and drove away, leaving the deputy staring after her and shaking his head.

Peggy focused her attention sharply on the road. The car floundered in the snow from time to time. The windshield wipers banged away frantically, but the snow kept on building up faster than they could clear it off. Peggy slowed down and peered through the windshield at the bottom edge where the defroster kept it clear. The headlights poked two dim yellow holes into the snow-mad darkness. The wind cried and whimpered in the trees.

Peggy's nerves were strained almost to breaking point. Then the car slid sideways. She jammed her foot down hard on the brake. The car went out of control, skating and skidding into the ditch.

Peggy turned off the ignition. She folded her arms over the steering wheel and rested her head against them. Her entire body trembled weakly.

What if the car had gone over the other side? She shuddered. What a stupid thing to do! Ram her foot down on the brake on icy roads! How could she do such a dumb thing?

She began to feel the cold. What was she going to do? She was far from the ranches and homes below, and she wasn't sure she could make it back to the ski resort. It had to be at least two miles away. But what if nobody came? Probably nobody would come tonight. Her family didn't even know she was coming home!

"I don't want to die, God," she begged. "I thought I did, but I don't. My little boy needs me."

She pulled herself together. What was it you were supposed to do when you got stranded in your car? Keep the exhaust pipe clear of snow. Crack the window for fresh air. And only run the engine for about ten minutes every hour.

Peggy zipped up her jacket, put on her gloves and tried to open the door. It was stuck—rammed against something. She slid across the seat to the other side and got out. The wind whipped the breath right out of her throat; it was colder than before, or maybe it only seemed to be colder here because across the narrow mountain road there was nothing... She shuddered again at the thought of falling into the canyon far below.

When she had cleared away the snow from the rear of the car, she climbed inside and huddled on the seat. She turned off the headlights and opened a window about an inch.

It was so dark. She shivered.

At 8:30 a pickup made its way down the narrow mountain road from the ski resort. Peggy saw the headlights and sat up quickly. She turned on her own lights so the person would know she was there. The pickup slowed and stopped. Peggy opened the door.

"You hurt?" a man asked.

"No. Just cold and scared."

The man got out and looked at the car. "It doesn't seem to be damaged much, but there's no way we can get it out tonight. Were you going to town?"

"Yes."

"Get in," he said. "I don't live in town, but if you don't mind stopping for a few minutes at my place so I can let my wife know what's going on I'll take you there."

"I could call my folks from your place and they could come and get me," she said, climbing up into the cab.

"Phones aren't working. It won't be any trouble for me to drive you into town."

"Thanks," she said. She buried her face in her hands and began to sob. "I'm sorry. I'm just so relieved."

"That's okay. Go ahead and get it all out. How long were you sitting there?"

"More than an hour."

"I bet you're half-frozen." He turned up the heater for her.

Peggy smiled gratefully, wiping her eyes dry with the back of her sleeve. On the dash in front of her she saw a metallic orange sticker that read: Jim Cord, Cord Electric. Thank you, Jim Cord, she breathed silently, for driving down this road tonight. And thank You, God, for letting him be here.

7

Jim Cord wheeled his pickup into the drive and glanced over at the girl. She was leaning her head against the door and her eyes were closed. Should he leave the truck running and just make a quick trip into the house to let Jan know what was going on? Blast it! He wished he didn't have to take her into town. He was about dead on his feet and his stomach churned with hunger. He hadn't had anything to eat since mid-morning. He was about to get out when the girl sat up.

"We're at my place," he said. "You can stay out here and wait or come on in, whichever you want. I'm starving. I thought I'd get my wife to make me a sandwich or something before we go into town."

She hesitated a moment. "I guess I could go in. You won't have to run the engine then."

They got out of the truck and went into the house. Janet came in from the living room.

"Jim! Where have you been? I've been worried . . ." She stopped, seeing the girl, and her face registered surprise.

Cord turned to the girl. "I don't know your name."

"Peggy Caldwell."

"This is my wife, Jan. Peggy's car went in the ditch up Snow Mountain Road. There was no way I could pull her out, so I thought I'd give her a ride into town."

Janet smiled politely. "Were you there long?"

Peggy nodded. "Long enough to be scared nobody would ever come. I'm sorry to be such a bother."

"That's okay. It's just a good thing Jim came along when he did. I don't imagine there'll be many people out driving in this storm."

"We should be going right away," Cord said. "Can I get you to make me a sandwich or two, Jan? I haven't eaten since I left this morning."

She nodded. "Have a chair by the fire, Peggy. By the way, this is Michael." She went into the kitchen, taking a candle with her. Cord followed. "What happened?" she asked. "You look exhausted."

"I am. It took all afternoon to repair the T-bar. By the time I got down to the chair lift the power had gone out. Arnie finally got me down to the lodge in the snowpacker. Then they needed help with their little generator so they could keep things going in the kitchen." He tried to rub the weariness from his eyes. "Where are the kids?"

"I guess they're at Brenners'. Right after you left, they took their sleds over. I fell asleep rocking Michael. His fever was up again. When I woke up it was all stormy outside. I tried to call over there, but the phones didn't work. I'm starting to get worried. I don't understand why Sid doesn't bring them home. Unless he's gone. I know Aggie wouldn't drive two feet in this storm."

"Maybe I'd better drive over there and bring them home before I go to town." He went to the door. "Peggy, two of my kids are stranded at a ranch up the road. Is your family expecting you at any certain time?"

She shook her head. "They don't expect me home at all tonight."

"Would you mind waiting awhile longer? I'd like to get the kids home."

"That'd be fine," she said. "I just wish I didn't have to bother you at all."

"No problem." He took the sandwiches and a can of pop from Jan, kissing her cheek. "Thanks, and don't worry. Everything's going to be all right."

He went back into the storm reluctantly and drove up the canyon road to Brenners'. At the door, he pushed the doorbell button before he remembered it wouldn't ring. He used his fist and banged hard.

Sid Brenner opened the door. "Come on in, come on in." He closed the door quickly behind Cord. "Isn't this some night!"

Cord was taken aback for a moment. Why

hadn't Brenner brought the kids home?

"Aggie, it's Jim Cord. Get him a cup of coffee." He motioned for Cord to follow him into the living room. "We've rigged up a stove of sorts in the fireplace. Come in and sit down."

Cord held up his hands in protest. "I can't stay. I came over to get the kids is all."

Aggie brought him a mug of coffee. "The kids?" she asked in surprise. "The kids aren't here."

"You mean they left for home?"

"We've been gone most of the day." Brenner said. "We didn't get back until dark. The kids haven't been here at all."

"Jan said they came over to play with their sleds. She assumed they were here at the house waiting."

"Oh, I'd have brought them home," Brenner said. "No, they haven't been here. They might have come and found us gone, and then gone out to the hill anyhow. You don't suppose they're still out there . . ."

Cord had an uneasy feeling in the pit of his stomach. "I don't know where else they'd go."

Aggie turned to her youngest son, Richie. He was a skinny kid with a mop of carrot-colored hair and a faceful of freckles. "Richie, do you know where Brian might have gone?"

He shook his head. "The only place I know is the sledding hill."

"He wouldn't have gone to anyone else's house?"

"Naw. All the other kids around here are way older than us."

Cord set down the mug. He felt sick all over with fear. "I've got to go find them." He headed for the door.

"Wait," Brenner said, taking his arm. "If they went to the hill they'd have cut through my land. The only way you'll find them is on a snowmobile. And you'll need help."

"We'll go," his two older sons offered.

"Me too," Richie said.

"Not you, Richie," his mother said. "It's too nasty out there."

"Dad?" he begged.

Brenner shook his head. "Not this time. We've got enough to worry about without worrying about you."

Richie threw himself into a chair and sulked angrily while Brenner and the two boys, Kevin and Randy, zipped up their snowmobile suits.

Aggie brought a helmet for Cord. "You're not dressed for this. I wish we had another suit."

"It doesn't matter," Cord said thickly. "All I care about is getting my kids."

"You will," she promised.

They went into the garage, uncovered the machines and started them up.

"I wish the phones were working," Cord said. "Jan will be worried when I don't get home."

"I could send one of the boys over."

"I don't know. . . . Maybe it'd be better if she didn't know. And the more of us there are looking, the sooner we'll find them."

"It's up to you."

Cord hesitated. What should he do? He looked at the Brenner boys. The oldest was fifteen or sixteen. He was hardly old enough to drive. What if something happened to him on the road? He shook his head slowly. "Let's just go look for the kids. We'll probably find them right away."

"Right," Brenner agreed. "I think I have a good idea where we'll find them. I have a couple of old sheds between here and the hill. They more than likely got caught in the storm or got tired of walking through the deep snow and crawled inside one of them."

The thought eased Cord's mind somewhat. The kids would be cold, but they'd be okay. Thank God.

They revved up the motors and rode into the yard.

"We'll spread out," Brenner shouted above the roar of the machines. "But we'll keep within sight of each other. We don't need to lose anyone else out there. And use your flashlights." He pointed to the compartment at the back of Cord's long, padded seat. "Flashlight."

They moved out of the yard, across the snow-buried cattleguard and into the trees, spreading out in a long line, side by side.

Cord probed the darkness with his flashlight, searching the drifts, the snow-heavy brush, the windfall and the trees. Please let us find them, he prayed. Let them be okay. He wished like crazy they were standing by the fire right this minute getting dried off and eating something hot and satisfying. His throat knotted up.

The wind bludgeoned them with icy snow and the darkness was absolute. They crouched on their knees, crawling with the machines over the snow, watching out for trees and hidden stumps that would jam them up.

"Over here!" Brenner yelled. His voice was swallowed up in the wind and roar of the machines, but the others saw that he had stopped and they joined him. He had found one of the sheds.

Cord stepped off his snowmobile, sinking groin-deep into the snow. He did the breast stroke with his arms and fought his way to the shed. He and Brenner struggled to open the drifted door. They ran their lights over the walls and floor space. The shed was empty.

"There are two more," Brenner said, gripping Cord's shoulder. "It won't be long before we have them."

"I don't know how they could have walked through these drifts," Cord said.

"They're a whole lot lighter than we are. There's a good crust about a foot down. I doubt that they broke through it. Besides, quite a bit of this just happened in the last few hours. I'm sure the kids found one of the sheds before it got dark. I know Richie likes to play in them when he's out here so Brian knows where they are."

Cord nodded. It sounded good. What bothered him was why Brian had waited so late before starting home. The kid had a watch. Had one of them been hurt?

They started out again, in search of the next shed. It was empty, and so was the third. They shut off their machines. For a moment no one spoke.

"Now what?" Cord asked finally. His brain was frozen with fear for his children. It would be so easy to get lost, to lose your bearings, especially in the darkness. He hardly had any sense of direction himself. It would have been terrible for the kids. They might have wandered around and around in circles and the snow would have kept erasing their tracks so they would never know. Brian was only eight. He was so little. . . .

"I guess we just move ahead," Brenner said slowly. "We'll cover every inch of ground between here and the hill." The doubt within him crept into his voice. "There are a hundred places where they could be holed up. Under some big old evergreen, in the brush, in some cranny in the rocks."

"How long do you think they can last out here?" Cord asked.

"It's hard to say. If they've found a good sheltered spot away from the wind, and if they aren't too wet, and if they huddle together . . . " He shook his head. "I don't know. It's not bad out of the wind. They could more than likely last all night." He started up his machine. "Let's hope and pray we find them, that's all."

Pray? Cord felt as if God had slammed the final door of the heavens shut in his face. He could no more pray than laugh. Why was it that every time he needed to pray he couldn't?

"You don't think we'll find them tonight, do you?" he said to Brenner.

"We'll find them," Brenner said abruptly, but he didn't sound so sure anymore.

Cord felt his fear grinding in the pit of his stomach. Why are You doing this to me? You can hurt me, You can take away my business and my life, but not my kids! He wanted to hammer his fist against the sky.

The storm was getting worse. The men and two boys huddled together, afraid of losing each other in the night. The snowmobiles whined and growled through the wet, heavy drifts.

Cord thought about taking a hot shower. He thought about food. The sandwiches hadn't filled him, and the hollow ache he had been feeling earlier returned, spreading out from his stomach to his arms and legs. He thought of Jan's hands working gently on that knot in his neck. She hadn't done that for weeks. He thought about stretching out on the couch. He thought of everything except Brian and Krissie out there somewhere.

Brenner surged ahead of the others. He swooped up suddenly over a sharp rise in the earth. Cord had his eyes glued on Brenner's tail light one second, and the next he was staring at nothing.

Drop-off! He braked cautiously, not wanting to

skid over the edge into the unknown. The boys came up beside him. Cord eased off his machine and shined his light over the snow.

They were on the rim of some kind of hollow. Brenner was below them about four or five yards. His machine lay on its side and he was half-pinned underneath it.

The three of them slid down the bank.

"You hurt, Dad?" Kevin asked.

Brenner was face down in the snow. He moved his arm and tried to lift his head. Blood was pouring from his nose.

Cord and the two boys pushed the machine upright. One of the skiis had broken off and the windshield was smashed.

Brenner rolled onto his back and sat up. He reached into his pocket for his handkerchief and held it over his nose.

"How badly are you hurt?" Cord asked.

"My arm," he said. "I don't think I broke it, but it hurts like fire." He wet the handkerchief in the snow and washed his face. "Nothing else hurts except my pride."

"The skiis are broken off your machine, Dad," Randy said.

"It figures. Well, you two kids can double up and I'll ride one of yours. We'll pick up my machine in the morning." He got up. "Come on. We'd better get going if we're planning to find those kids."

As they climbed up the bank to the snowmobiles, Cord made up his mind. "We're calling it quits," he said. His throat was all jammed up with hurt at having to say it. "We're not going to find them tonight. We can't even see where we're going, much less hunt for them."

"You aren't worried about me, are you?" Brenner asked. "Listen, buddy, I'm okay. I've piled up dozens of times. It's no big deal."

Cord swallowed the lump in his throat and shook his head firmly. "No," he said. "Somebody could really get hurt next time. I'll drive into town tonight and get help."

"We want to come along," Brenner said. "The more guys you have looking the sooner you'll find them."

"Maybe the kids already got home," Randy said.

The two men looked at him and then at each other. "It's possible," Brenner said slowly. "If they took the shortcut instead of the road you wouldn't have passed them on your way over to our place."

"They probably got home right after you left!" Kevin said with enthusiasm. "We should have checked first. How come we never even thought of it?"

Cord felt the hope surging back into him. That was undoubtedly what had happened. Now the only thing he had to face when he got home was Janet's worried anger. He shone the light on his watch. It was nearly 10:00!

"If we head straight right, we should come out

on the road," Brenner said. "It'll be easy from there."

The machines roared up.

"I'll break trail," Cord shouted. "Yell if I get off course." He moved ahead of the others. Now that some of the worry and fear had eased out of him, he began to ache with his tiredness. His arms hurt intensely around the shoulders from hauling the heavy snowmobile out of deep, wet drifts and manipulating it through trees and brush.

They came at last to the road.

8

Deputy Sheriff Mitch Rettick had finished his investigation of a shooting incident at Snow Mountain Ski Resort within an hour after he arrived there. It had been nothing more than an argument between a husband and wife who had both had too much wine for their honeymoon celebration. They hadn't offered much information and he had been unable to find any evidence of a gun. Either the neighbors had heard something else or imagined it, or the couple was covering for each other and they had hidden the gun. In any case, everything was quiet and under control by the time he got there.

His shift had ended hours ago, but he had offered to go on call tonight because of the coming storm. And because he didn't want to go home.

He decided to get something to eat before leaving the resort. They served an excellent steak dinner here, and he hadn't eaten much lunch.

"Are they serving meals in the dining room?" he asked someone.

"Yeah. They've got electricity in there—in the kitchen I mean. They're serving everything on the menu."

Rettick went downstairs to the dining area, finding a small table in the corner. The place was packed with people. The service would probably be slow. Well, he didn't mind. Anything was better than going home these days.

An attractive blond waitress brought a menu. "It'll be awhile," she said, smiling. "I hope you don't mind."

"I don't mind at all," he said, returning her smile. He wished she had time to talk.

"Can I bring you some coffee?" she asked. "Or a drink?"

"Coffee would be fine." He watched her walk away to the counter, then opened the menu.

She returned with the coffee. "Can I take your order now?"

"I'll have the rib steak, rare."

"How would you like your potato?"

"Baked, with sour cream."

"Dressing?"

"French."

"I think we're out of that tonight. I'm sorry."

"Thousand Island then."

She read the order back to him. "Okay?"

"Fine." He lit a cigarette, leaned back and closed his eyes, smoking slowly and thinking.

A kind of inner tension had been building up inside him for months now, like water backed up behind a dam. It had nothing to do with his failing marriage or with the pressures of his job, although both added to it. There was nothing wrong, at least nothing he could put his finger on, except this blasted restlessness he had been feeling lately.

He stubbed out his cigarette and lit another one, sipping absently at his coffee. It burned his mouth and throat, and bothered his empty stomach. He set the cup down and sucked on his cigarette.

What was bugging him? His age, maybe? He'd be forty in a few weeks. He had to admit he didn't like the idea. But it was more than that. Maybe it had something to do with the fact that he had attained all his goals and now he had nothing left to work for. He had married the woman he had once loved passionately. He had become a cop. He had made good money—good enough anyhow—and he had a new home, two cars, snowmobiles, a boat, a modest cabin at the lake. And he had two terrific kids. He had everything a man could want.

But it wasn't everything he had expected it to be.

And now he had run out of dreams. He was a middle-aged man and he had nowhere to go. He wished he could be a kid again. Kids live on dreams of tomorrow. Tomorrow they will do this and tomorrow they will be that. They lie awake at night and dream and plan of how it will be so wonderful for them when they grow up.

Then they grow up, and maybe they fulfill their childhood dreams and maybe they don't. But as soon as they grow up, they stop dreaming because dreams aren't enough to live on.

He wouldn't have believed that it could happen to him, but here he was, restless and bored and empty.

What had he thought? That becoming a cop would make him into some kind of god? When he was a kid, six years old, he was lost once, in downtown Chicago. A cop found him standing on the edge of the swarming crowds, crying, and took him to his car and drove him around the block until he found his parents. He showed him his siren and his radio and his gun, and he gave him a pair of handcuffs to keep as a souvenir. From that day on, he worshipped cops and vowed that when he got old enough he was going to be one.

It didn't take him long to discover that cops were the same as ordinary people and that not everybody worshipped them. In a way, though, cops and God did have a lot in common when it came to the way people treated them. Both cops and God were supposed to stick around, but only in the background, out of the way, until the exact moment they were needed. And then, like magic, they were supposed to appear on the scene, not a second too late, and they were supposed to know and solve and fix everything with no mistakes.

It wasn't that he didn't like being a cop. He did.

He wouldn't want to be anything else. It was just that being one wasn't all he had dreamed it would be. It hadn't been able to fulfill him. He still felt there was something lacking—something he couldn't find. It was like a hunger, not in the pit of his stomach, but in his soul. It was a thing he didn't understand. What was it about a man that he could have almost everything and still want more?

The waitress set his meal in front of him. "I really am sorry it took so long."

"I'm in no hurry," he said. "I'm off duty, actually."

"Thanks for waiting." She refilled his cup. "Is there anything else I can get for you?"

"This'll be fine."

The steak was exactly right: red on the inside, seared on the outside, and smothered in fresh mushrooms. Rettick ate slowly, relishing every bite and not thinking, just enjoying his meal.

He finished, and lit another cigarette, waiting for the sherbet that came with the order. He was smoking more and more these days, probably because of that blasted tension he was carrying around inside. It was becoming a part of his body, tensing his facial muscles and keeping him awake nights.

He left a generous tip, paid at the counter and went outside. The storm had gotten much worse. The road was thick with snow. He wondered if he ought to chain up the jeep. It might be the best way.

He laid the chains out carefully behind the rear tires, then backed up over them. He got out, hooking them around the wheels securely. He would have no trouble getting down the mountain now. He called the office. There was no answer. Too much interference.

The jeep was warm and moved easily down the winding mountain road without sliding, the chains crunching into the ice and gripping it strongly.

He saw something, it looked like a car, under a thin mound of snow, in the ditch. He stopped and went over to it, clearing away the snow from the windshield. It was pitch black inside. He found the door handle. The door was frozen shut, but he yanked on it until it opened. The car was empty. He cleared away more snow. It was that young girl's car, he was sure of it. So she had gone off the road after all. He had thought she probably would. He saw the suitcase in the back seat. Surely she hadn't tried to walk for help.

He drove slowly, worrying his way along the road, watching for signs of the girl. If she had fallen, he would never see her. He hoped someone had come along and given her a ride. But why hadn't she taken her suitcase?

He had gone another three miles when he saw lights coming up out of the trees. Snowmobiles? Who on earth would be out in weather like this? They must have had some trouble. He stopped, rolling down his window, and waited for them to come alongside him.

"Hello. I saw your lights and thought I'd see if you need help or anything."

"I'm not sure whether we need help or not," one of the men said. "We're out looking for two little kids. My wife says they brought their sleds out here. When I got home awhile ago, the kids still weren't back. She thought they were at the neighbor's. But they weren't."

"You think they're out here?"

"We did. We've been out here since, what time was it? About 8:30 I think. We think now that the kids took the shortcut between our two houses instead of the road, and we missed them." A small piece of fear still lay at the bottom of his mind. "If they're not at home," he said, "I'll need help in the morning."

The deputy nodded. "Why don't I follow you to the house," he suggested. "If the kids aren't there, I'll report it in town and get a search party going as soon as it's light."

"That reminds me. I picked up a young woman whose car went off the road. She's at the house waiting for me to get home and give her a ride to town."

"Pretty girl with dark hair?"

"Yeah."

"That's good to know. I warned her about the road before she left the lodge. She was insistent about leaving. When I saw her car in the ditch, I was afraid she had tried walking for help. I've been watching for a sign of her. She was lucky. I'll take her into town for you."

"I'd appreciate that," the man said. He eased out ahead of the jeep.

Rettick rolled up his window and followed the snowmobiles. He hoped like blazes those kids were at home. He got a sick feeling in his gut whenever something happened to a kid, maybe because his own kids meant more to him than anything else in his life. It was his kids that kept him from wiggling out of his infernal trap of a marriage.

He briefly recalled last night's fight, when finally their cold war had exploded into the ugly, irrevocable words they had both been choking back for months. In the end, Valerie had threatened to take the kids and leave him. She could do it, she said, because of the affair he had had and her proof of it.

He didn't care about losing her. What they had shared once had long since been dead. He felt nothing for her. But those kids, they were the best part of his life. Losing them would be like losing a part of himself.

They turned onto the canyon road to the first house. Rettick saw the curtains part, and someone looked out. Man, he hoped those kids were home. He watched the man he had talked with earlier go inside.

Janet met Cord at the door. She glanced past him. "Where have you been? Where are the kids?"

"They didn't make it home?"

"What do you mean, they didn't make it

home?" She stood perfectly still, her face white. "Jim . . ."

"The kids never went to Brenners'. Or at least, Brenners weren't home all day. We've been out looking for them. It was useless. We couldn't see anything. Brenner got hurt. We got to thinking maybe the kids had cut across the field instead of using the road to our house. We were hoping . . ." His voice broke. They stared at each other with silent misery.

"What are we going to do?"

"There's nothing we can do except wait for daylight."

"We can't leave them out there all night!" Jan cried.

Cord gripped his wife's arms firmly. "We don't have any other choice, Jan. It's unbelievably dark out there and the storm is getting steadily worse. It's like hunting for a needle in a haystack. Brenner already got hurt. Luckily it wasn't serious. Next time it could be. We have to wait until we can see. I don't like it any better than you do." His chest filled with his agony. "We think the kids are holed up somewhere. As long as they're in a sheltered spot they should be okay. Brian's got a good head on his shoulders. He'll take care of his sister."

"I'm so scared, Jim."

"I know. So am I." They held each other tightly for a long moment. "I've got to get Peggy," Jim said finally. "We met a cop on the way back. He's going to take her into town for me. He's also going to get Search and Rescue out here first thing in the morning." He went into the living room. "Peggy?"

She got up from her chair.

"There's a deputy sheriff waiting outside to take you home. He says he saw you at the ski resort."

She was embarrassed. "He told me he thought I should leave in the morning because the road was so bad."

They went outside to where the others waited. At the question in their faces, Cord shook his head. "They aren't there."

"Is Jan holding up okay?" Brenner asked.

"She took it pretty well. She's upset and scared."

"There's no point in your going to get your pickup tonight," Brenner said. "You stay home with Jan. We'll be coming back to help as soon as it's daylight anyhow. We'll bring the pickup then."

"How about your arm?"

"Don't worry about my arm. Finding those kids is more important than avoiding a little pain. We'll leave the machine here for you. See you tomorrow."

Cord nodded and waved gratefully as Brenner and his two boys rode away. Peggy climbed into the jeep with Rettick. The deputy stuck his hand through the open window.

"I don't know your name."

"Cord. Jim Cord."

"Mitch Rettick. We'll get your kids for you,"

he promised. "You know what general area they would be in?"

"Yes, I think so."

"You checked with other families up the canyon?"

"They don't know anyone else besides Brenners and that's where they were headed, according to my wife. Brenners have a big hill that's perfect for sledding. The kids go there quite often."

"I see. How old are they?"

"Brian is eight. Krissie is five. Or maybe she's six now. I can't keep track."

Young. Terribly young. "Your son—do you think he might have looked for shelter?"

"I'm banking on that," Cord said. "We checked the old sheds on Brenner's property in that area. But they could have crawled under a tree like the deer do."

"I hope so." Rettick shook his hand again. "Try to get some rest tonight. I know it won't be easy. We'll have the place swarming with men tomorrow. I'll try to get a helicopter in here too if it clears up enough." He shifted into reverse. "See you in the morning." He backed out of the drive and drove around the corner and out of sight.

The roads to Snow Mountain Ski Resort and Rock Creek Canyon had been carved into opposite sides of the same mountain. Approximately two miles before the roads branched off to circle the mountain, there was a steep slope that fell sharply from the sky to the road, and from the road to the river bottom. The slope was covered with loose, dangerous shale and tangles of windfall.

For days the snow had piled up and piled up until the shale began to shift uneasily beneath its load.

Suddenly the face of the mountain dropped off.

Snow and rock and windfall thundered downward in one massive, violent, twisting, heaving, wrenching cataclysmic wave. It burst out over the road and roared on down the slope below, rending trees from the ground, pulverizing the rock and shattering shale into thousands of tiny fragments. A gigantic snowcloud mushroomed into the air like smoke from an A-bomb explosion.

Then, in seconds, it was over. The roar died away. The earth stopped its awful shuddering and the snowcloud settled gently into the earth.

The wind returned, tearing cruelly at the gutted, devastated mountainside. The snow came again and laid a thin white sheet over it.

Less than five minutes later, Mitch Rettick rounded a bend in the road. His mouth gaped.

"What the—!"

He stopped his jeep and jumped out. The road had been utterly obliterated, wiped out, buried under a ton of snow and debris. He was certain it had just happened, and the thought that he and the girl could have been underneath all that mess left him weak.

He didn't really believe in God, although he did believe in the existence of some tremendous controlling Force in the universe, but at that moment he felt that there should be Someone personal and reachable for him to thank.

Rettick got into his jeep, rubbing his chin thoughtfully. He wouldn't get home tonight. That was no big deal. But he had to get Search and Rescue. He tried the radio. There was nothing. He swore, then remembered the girl.

She was watching him. "Looks like we'll be stuck here for awhile," she said. "How long do you think?"

"I don't know. First someone will have to discover the avalanche—someone on the outside—and then report it. After that it'll depend on how extensive the damage is. I can't tell in the dark."

"So we could be here for days."

"Possibly." He found a cigarette and lit it. "I imagine by now your family is pretty worried. Maybe they'll try to find you tonight."

"No. I was supposed to stay about a week. They didn't expect me home."

He swore again. He was going to have to tell Cord and his wife. He would have given anything to be able to drive out of this blasted mess and forget the whole thing.

"You're worried about those kids, aren't you?" she said softly. "You don't think they'll find them without help, do you?"

"There's a lot of country out there and this

storm isn't getting any better." He wheeled the jeep around angrily in the narrow road and started up the canyon toward the Cords' home. The girl beside him was silent, knowing the fresh agony they would be facing, and hating the snow that sometimes made people die.

Part Three

9

Cord and his wife lay close together on the couch in front of the fire.

"Are you okay? Cord asked.

"I don't know."

"I've been thinking about how some people live every day of their lives this way."

She turned her face toward him. "What way?"

"In fear for their own lives or the lives of those they love."

"Oh."

"I guess knowing that there are others who are hurting as much or more than we are doesn't really help though."

"No," she said, "it doesn't."

"This morning all I could think about was my business and the unpaid bills and the house. Now it doesn't even matter. I'd trade everything I own to get my kids back home safely." His voice choked up.

"I know."

Cord got up and put more wood on the fire. He lay beside Janet again and pulled the afghan over them. It was getting colder. He could feel it through the walls and around the windows. He hoped Jan wouldn't notice.

"Do you think they're sleeping?" she asked suddenly.

"I think so."

"It's so cold."

"I know, but I'm sure they're curled up in some nice sheltered spot."

"Zane is with them."

"That's good. He'll keep them warm."

They lay quietly, staring into the fire, thinking about their children and waiting for the morning. In Brian and Krissie's rooms, Peggy Caldwell and Mitch Rettick slept restlessly.

It was still dark when Janet got up and set the table for breakfast. She filled the table with boxes of cold cereal, bread, milk, orange juice and a jar of canned peaches, wishing she could make something hot.

"I'm going with you," she said as Cord came into the kitchen.

"No."

"Yes I am! I can't sit around here waiting and wondering. Peggy Caldwell can stay with Michael."

"There aren't enough machines for you."

"I could double with you."

"No. It'd slow us down, that's all."

"I can't stay here."

He took her face between his hands. "You can and you will because you have to. And you'll be strong because the kids will need their mother when they get home."

Rettick came into the kitchen, clearing his throat to let them know he was there. He could see immediately that neither of them had slept.

Janet turned away abruptly and started hauling things out of the refrigerator. "I'll make a lunch," she said.

"That's a good idea," Cord said, sitting at the table. "Maybe you should throw in some sandwiches for Brenner and his boys." He motioned at Rettick to sit down. "I imagine Brenners will bring three machines this morning, and I have one. The boys can ride double again so you can ride one of theirs."

Janet glared at him accusingly.

"The boys are smaller than you and me together," he told her. "And they're used to riding. You aren't." He turned to the deputy. "She wants to go along."

"It won't be much fun out there, Mrs. Cord," Rettick said gently. "Actually the best thing you could do for your kids would be to have some warm food waiting. Hot soup or hot tea would be best. And you should have plenty of lukewarm water."

Jan stared at him. "How can I do that?" she asked. "There's no electricity, the water pipes are frozen."

"Get snow and boil it. You should be able to rig something up over the fire."

"The camping stove is out in the garage," Cord said. "We have those old kettles too, that we use for camping. I'll go out and get them for you."

Rettick shook his head. "Let her get them later. She'll need to keep occupied."

"Can you light it?" Cord asked her.

"Yes, I think so."

"It should have plenty of propane."

"Do you have any old blankets we can take along, Mrs. Cord?"

She nodded.

"We'll need those to warm the kids with."

"You think they'll be suffering from frostbite, don't you?" Cord said when she had gone to find the blankets. "I noticed how much the temperature dropped during the night."

There was a loud knock at the door. "Brenner." Cord got up and let them in.

"I see the sheriff is back," Brenner said, stomping his boots and rubbing the warmth into his hands. "Did he get hold of Search and Rescue?"

"They never made it to town last night," Cord said quietly. "An avalanche wiped out the road below the fork. We've been completely sealed off from the outside."

"Oh man!" Brenner took off his hat. "We sure

could have used the help. It's bad out there. Can't see more than a couple of feet in front of your nose. It's a heap colder too. Almost ten below."

Cord whistled softly. "Don't say anything to Jan about the temperature. She's got enough to worry about as is. I don't think she could handle anything else."

"I understand."

They joined Rettick in the kitchen.

"This is Sid Brenner and his boys, Kevin and Randy. Deputy Sheriff Rettick. I don't recall your first name."

"Mitch." He extended his hand politely.

Have you eaten breakfast?" Cord asked them.

"Yeah. Aggie sent along a couple of thermoses of hot coffee and some sandwiches."

Jan returned with the blankets. "Are these okay?"

"Perfect."

"Aggie said to tell you she'd be thinking of you today. She wanted to come along, but she wasn't feeling well."

"Nothing serious, I hope," Cord said.

"Just a touch of the flu. She felt pretty bad about not being able to come. She figured you could use the company."

"The girl I picked up last night is here," Cord said.

The morning had lightened to a dull gray. Cord found an extra pair of long underwear for the deputy. The men dressed warmly and Jan brought scarves for their necks and faces.

"Hang in there," Cord said, taking her in his arms. "I love you."

"I love you too."

"Pray for us," he said.

She nodded and let him go.

"I have an idea," Kevin said as they went outside. "Randy and I could try to get past the avalanche on the snowmobile."

"I don't know . . ." Brenner looked at the deputy. "How bad is it?"

"I couldn't tell in the dark."

"We could do it, Dad! I know we could. We could go down, cross the creek, go up along the other side and back to the road. All we'd have to do is get to the first ranch. We need help, Dad."

"Yes, we do need help. All right, you can go. But stick to the road. I don't want you getting lost."

"I don't know," Cord said. "What if they trigger another avalanche?"

"I don't think they will," Rettick said, "as long as they're careful."

"We will be," Kevin promised.

"I wish there were some other way," Cord said.

"There isn't," Brenner told him. "Kevin, if it looks like it's too dangerous, I want you to turn around and go home. I expect you to use your head. And I don't want you trying to find us. Do you understand?"

"Yes, Dad."

"No shortcuts, no playing around."

"Yes, Dad."

He gave both their shoulders a squeeze. "We'll see you later then."

They warmed up their snowmobiles. "Maybe we should check the shortcut between our place and yours," Cord shouted above the roaring motors.

"That's what I thought."

"We're leaving, Dad," Kevin shouted. The two boys moved out onto the road and were swallowed up by the blowing snow.

Cord looked after them doubtfully. If anything happened to them he would never forgive himself for letting them go. He pushed the thought into the back of his mind and gave his full attention to the search that lay ahead of them. He squeezed the throttle in his right hand, steering the big machine across his yard.

The men zig-zagged slow swaths back and forth across the land that lay between the two houses, searching the fence line and the trees and the ditches, and prodding the deep drifts. They found no sign of the children and their dog.

Finally Brenner signalled Cord and Rettick to follow him to the sledding hill to search the area they had searched the night before.

The wind howled through the canyon, pounding the trees and hurling snow into the sky. The cold was beginning to cut through their clothes; their faces were red and half-paralyzed. The vapor from their breath got caught in their eyebrows and froze into tiny white beads there. They pulled their scarves over the lower parts of their faces and tried to keep behind the windshields as much as possible. The trouble with that was they couldn't see where they were going.

They circled through the trees, checking the sheds and all around them in case they had missed something in the darkness, but there was nothing. Even the signs of their own search had been rubbed out by the drifting snow.

The wind grew stronger. It was getting impossible to see. They stayed together, no more than a foot apart. Rettick almost smacked into the corner of a shed.

"Another shed!" he yelled.

Brenner waved his hand negatively. "We're going in circles," he shouted. "Let's break here."

They shut off their machines and entered the little shed. Brenner opened the bag of sandwiches and poured some coffee. The hot liquid warmed their cold-stiffened hands through the thin styrofoam cups.

"It's no use," Cord said finally. He dropped his head into his hands. "We're not going to find them until this storm quits."

The other two men looked at him helplessly.

"How am I going to tell Jan?" He looked up at the deputy. "We won't find them alive, will we?"

"People have survived colder temperatures for longer periods of time than this," Rettick said.

"But not kids. Those were adults who knew what to do."

"Not necessarily. Some of them did nothing except lie down and wait to die."

"Don't give up hope yet," Brenner said.

Cord closed his eyes. Whatever wrongs I've done, please don't make my children suffer for them, he prayed silently. Take care of them, I beg of You.

It was the only thing left to do, and his faith in God was so weak he wasn't sure it could hold him up. But it was still the only thing left to do.

Sometime during the morning, Brian was awakened by a crashing sound. Zane barked and yelped wildly above them. Krissie sat up, rubbing her eyes.

It was pitch black in the cellar except for the thin crack of light at the opening where Brian had jammed the hunk of wood. He felt around him, trying to figure out where they were.

Then he remembered. Krissie started wailing and the dog barked even louder. Brian stuck his fingers into his ears.

"Shut up!" he yelled. "You're driving me crazy!"

It got quiet again, except for the wind shrieking outside. Brian struggled to get up. His feet hurt badly. He could hardly stand to walk on them. He found the ladder and climbed it slowly. He reached over his head and pushed on the trap door. He couldn't get it open. Zane poked his nose through the crack and whined, licking Brian's mittens.

Brian clung to the ladder. He was tired and hungry and cold. He wanted to cry. He wanted to be home. Why didn't Dad come and get them? But how silly. Dad would never find them here. He didn't even know about this place.

They had to get out of here. It was morning now and they would be able to see. They had to get home. They just had to.

He shoved at the door again. This time it gave way a little. But that was all. What was the matter? It was not supposed to be hard to lift the door.

Then suddenly he knew. The snow had caved in more of the ceiling right on top of them. They were buried down in the cellar and nobody knew where they were and they were going to die here.

"No! No! No!" The next thing he knew he was yelling and screaming and pounding like a crazy person at the door.

"Brian! Brian!" Krissie screamed below him. "Brian, what's the matter! Stop it! You're scaring me!" She stood at the bottom of the ladder, jerking frantically at his legs.

Brian felt himself falling. He clutched at the ladder and caught it. He held himself steady, rubbing his sleeve across his eyes and nose. "Let go of me, you dummy! You almost made me fall."

Krissie backed away. "Why are you screaming?"

"I'm not screaming anymore," he said. "Just be quiet so I can think."

"Well, why aren't we getting out?"

"Because some wood and stuff fell on the door and I can't push it up, that's why."

"I don't want to stay here! I want to go home."

"Krissie! I can't think when you're hollering!"

"I want to get out!"

"Well, I'm trying to figure out what to do!" He leaned his head back, and looked at the trap door. If he only wasn't so hungry and cold he could probably get it open in a minute. He gathered up all his strength and shoved again. He heard something shift, and felt the door open several inches more. "I almost got it!" he shouted. He tried to squeeze through, but the opening was not big enough.

He climbed down, dropping wearily to the ground.

"Aren't we going?" Krissie asked.

"I'm tired. I have to rest for a minute." He leaned against the wall. He wished he weren't the oldest. He wished Krissie were a boy so she could do something. He wished . . . Oh, how were they going to get home?

"Krissie," he said, "you're going to have to walk home. I can't pull you on the sled anymore."

"But the snow's too deep!"

"I can't pull you, that's all there is to it. You can walk right behind me in my tracks. We'll leave the toboggan and the shovels here."

"Mom and Dad will be mad."

"I don't care. I'm too tired to take all that stuff." He had an idea. "Maybe you could get through the door if I hold it up. Then you could pull some of the wood off it."

"I can't do that! It's too heavy."

"It is not. It's probably little pieces. Besides, all you have to do is move it a tiny bit. Just enough so I can get out too. Come on, Krissie. I can't do everything."

"Okay."

"You climb the ladder first and I'll get behind you and hold the door open."

As Krissie wiggled through, Brian felt the door open another inch.

"We're getting it! We're getting it!"

"There's a great big board on top of it and a bunch of other stuff."

"Well try to get the little stuff off then." He heard Krissie working above him, and finally he was able to get his head and arms through. The door felt heavy on his back. "Hold it for me."

Krissie squatted down and lifted the door, and Brian crawled out. He lay on the floor for a moment.

"Get up, Brian."

He stood up reluctantly. "I wish we were already home."

"Me too."

"I'm so hungry I could eat the whole house."

Krissie giggled. "Me too." She took his hand.

The wind outside was terrible. The two children gasped for breath, fighting to stay on their feet.

The dog whimpered anxiously. The drift piled against the house was as high as Brian's chest. His legs buckled under him. The tears spilled out all over his face.

"We have to go back," he sobbed. Somehow he got up from the snow and staggered into the house. His teeth were rattling and his hands were shaking with the cold.

Krissie was crying again. "Aren't we ever going home again?"

"Dad will come and get us," Brian said. "I bet he's already on his way." He could hardly talk right. The words sounded funny, like a drunk man he had heard once. If only he could build a fire. There was lots of wood he could use. But there weren't any matches and he was too tired anyhow. He wanted to go back to the root cellar. It was warmer there because the wind couldn't get them.

"We have to go down again," he told his sister.

"I don't like it down there."

"It's the best place," Brian argued weakly.

"You have to leave the door open then."

"Okay."

The children climbed into the cellar. Zane whined and fussed above them.

"Come on, Zane," Krissie coaxed. "It's not very far for you to jump. You can do it. Come on."

The dog circled the hole, barking with frustration.

"Here Zane," Brian called.

Zane crouched at the edge. Then he jumped, knocking the children against the wall. They hugged him.

"I hope Dad gets here soon," Krissie whimpered.

The children lay down in the fetal position, huddling together, seeking each other's warmth. Brian tried to wrap the tarp over them, but his frozen weak fingers couldn't grasp it and it slipped away from him. He clamped both hands over a corner of it and brought it around them.

"My hands hurt," Krissie complained.

"Open your snowsuit a little bit and stick your hands inside under your arms. That's what Dad always tells me to do when I get really cold."

Zane curled up against them.

Brian closed his eyes. At least his feet didn't hurt anymore. He couldn't even feel them.

His thoughts were getting more and more mixed up. Dad was coming. He would find them soon. But Dad didn't know about this place. How could he find them here? Dad thought he was at Richie Brenner's sledding hill. But Richie Brenner knew about this place. He could tell Dad. Only he wouldn't know they were here. And maybe they wouldn't even ask him anyhow.

He never should have lied. He should have told Mom where they were going. But he couldn't do that. She wouldn't have let him go and then he wouldn't have that money for Dad. But what if Dad never found him? Then he would never get his money.

His breath came out in little sobs. Maybe God wanted them to be dead so Dad wouldn't have to use his money to take care of them. But God loved them. He wouldn't want to let them die.

He never should have said those mean things to Dad about how he wished he lived with Richie and his dad. What if Dad couldn't find them and they died? Then his dad would never know he loved him and didn't mean all that stuff. Maybe God was mad at him for lying and being bad and always begging for stuff his dad couldn't buy. He felt so scared.

Then he remembered how his mom had told him once how God was his Father, and that He loved him even more than Dad loved him, and that He would always forgive him and love him no matter how many bad things he did. Just like Dad, only even better.

"I'm sorry," he half-whispered. "Please don't be mad at me, Jesus." He felt the tears working up in his eyes and this time he didn't bother to blink them away.

He thought about Jesus and Heaven. Mom said it was a wonderful place—more wonderful than anyone could ever imagine. He knew he would never be hungry there, or cold, and he wouldn't hurt either.

But Mom and Dad wouldn't be there. More than anything he wanted to be with them. His body shook with sobs.

"What's the matter?" Krissie asked.

"Nothing. I'm just cold."

Krissie snuggled closer to him. "Don't worry, Brian. Jesus will take care of us until Dad comes."

She didn't know that Dad might never come. He thought about Richie. Please ... let ... Richie ... tell ... He thought about Heaven. How did you get there? Would they just disappear and Mom and Dad would never know where they went? Maybe Jesus would tell them. He didn't have to be afraid. Jesus would take care of them. He drifted off to sleep.

Beside the children, Zane lifted his head from time to time and whined softly, then dropped his head on his paws again. After awhile he didn't lift his head anymore.

10

After the men left that morning, Janet stood at the window, parting the drapes and peering outside. On a normal day, she could see almost to Brenners' house except for the thick grove of trees that grew around it. Today she couldn't see across their own yard. She knew the men were out there, only a short distance from her, searching the snow for her children.

Peggy Caldwell came into the kitchen, startling her. "They've gone?"

"Yes." She began to stack dirty dishes in the sink. "Help yourself to whatever you want."

Peggy sat down and poured a bowl of cereal. "How's your little boy?"

"He's still sleeping. He didn't wake up at all last night. He seems to be better."

"Did he have the flu?"

"I don't know. He does that sometimes. Gets a fever for a day or two and then he's okay. I don't know what it is."

"My little boy does that too. It must be a thing babies go through."

"I didn't realize you were married."

"I'm a widow," Peggy said abruptly.

"I'm sorry. How old is your boy?"

"A year and a half. His name is Roddie."

Janet looked closely at the girl. Her child was still a baby. She couldn't have been widowed long then.

"I miss him like crazy and I've only been gone two days," Peggy said. "I used to hear mothers talk about missing their kids and think they were awfully weird. Now I'm one of them. This is the first time I've been away from him." She poured milk over her cereal. "Does it get easier as they get older?"

"It's always hard, but I guess it does get easier. But they're a part of you. You can't ever stand to lose them." Her voice trailed off into a whisper.

"I'm sorry," Peggy said. "I didn't mean to remind you."

Janet pulled herself together. "I have to go out to the garage," she said. "That cop told me to make a hot drink and to heat some water for the kids."

"For frostbite," Peggy said. "You want to warm them as soon as possible."

"I thought you were supposed to rub them with ice or snow. I thought it was dangerous to thaw a frostbitten part quickly."

Peggy shook her head. "If the exposure has

been relatively short, rapid thawing of the tissues results in less loss of tissue than does slow thawing. And you never, never rub the area with ice or snow."

"You sound like a nurse."

"I am."

"Really?" Janet thought about how both a police officer and a nurse had been stranded at her home. Was it a coincidence or had God planned it that way? "I'm so glad you and Mr. Rettick are here with us. We would have done all the wrong things. Can they live through this?" she asked suddenly.

"It's possible," Peggy told her. "Especially if they find them right away. They might hardly be frostbitten at this point. Most frostbite occurs at temperatures below freezing, and it wasn't that cold yesterday."

"That's true," Janet said. "Well, I should get that stuff from the garage. There's no telling how soon they'll be back. They think the kids might be right in this area."

"Do you need some help?"

"No, I don't think so. But Michael might wake up while I'm gone."

"I'll take care of him."

"Thanks." Janet pulled on her jacket, tied the hood around her face, and put on her boots and gloves. As she opened the door and stepped outside, she gasped. It was freezing cold! Much colder than yesterday. Fear spread through her. When had the temperature dropped? What if they didn't find the kids right away?

She went into the garage. It was black inside. She had forgotten there was no electricity; she hadn't brought a flashlight. She walked to the car and found one under the driver's seat. She shone the light over the shelves. The camping gear was stacked neatly in the back corner. Janet rummaged through it quickly, stamping her feet to keep them warm.

How could they get through this? How could they live through a whole night of such cold? She was shivering after a few minutes in a sheltered garage. They were out there in the middle of the storm. She fought the rising hysteria in her throat and carried the camp stove, a bucket and a fireblackened coffee pot into the house. Without stopping to take off her coat, she unfolded the stove and started it up. Blue fire ringed the burners. She lowered the flame, then extinguished it.

"I'll have to get some snow," she said to Peggy. "I can't get used to not having things like water and electricity."

She ladled new snow from the top with a kettle until the bucket was packed with it. She lugged it into the kitchen and scooped some of the snow into a large kettle and some of it into the coffee pot. She set them on the burners and lit the stove again.

When the snow had melted, she added more, and then filled the basket of the coffee pot with grounds and put the lid on it.

Michael stumbled sleepily into the room. "I'm hungry."

"What do you want?" she asked, lifting him into her arms.

He glanced briefly around the table. "Peaches and cream," he said.

"Are you sure?"

"Yep."

She spooned several peach halves into a small dish and chopped them into tiny pieces. She poured milk over them. Then she set him in his chair. When he had finished eating, she helped him dress and she brought some of his favorite toys into the living room near the fire.

"I want to go outside with Brian and Krissie," he said. "I want to make a snowman."

"Brian and Krissie aren't home, sweetheart."

"Is it a school day?"

"No."

He went to the TV and turned it on. "It doesn't work, Mommy. Fix it."

"I can't. There's no electricity to make it work."

"Well what can I do?"

"I don't have anybody to play with me," Peggy said. "My little boy is home and I miss him."

"Is he bigger than me?" Michael asked.

"No. He's not three yet. He's not even two. His name is Roddie."

"Can he do puzzles?"

"Not yet."

"I can. Do you want to do one with me?"

"Sure. That'd be fun."

Janet returned to the kitchen. The coffee thumped in the pot; its rich aroma spread into the air.

"Would you like some coffee?" she called.

"That sounds wonderful."

"Cream or sugar?"

"Black."

Janet filled a mug and took it to Peggy. She filled a mug for herself. She looked with disgust at the mess. She poured half the hot water from the kettle into the dishpan, adding more snow to keep it full.

When the water had cooled enough, she washed the dishes. Using more water from the kettle, she rinsed them and placed them in the drying rack. She decided to dry them and put them away. She kept going to the window to see if they were coming.

She wandered into the living room.

"Look what we made," Michael said showing off a tottering tower of blocks.

"That's nice," she said. She picked a magazine off the cherry-wood coffee table. She thumbed through it. She couldn't get interested in the articles. She tossed it aside. She threw more wood on the fire. She went to the window and watched the storm. She looked at her watch every few minutes.

The sobbing of the wind in the trees filled her ears. She pressed her hands against the glass and felt the cold. She shivered.

"If only I hadn't fallen asleep yesterday," she said suddenly. "Then I would have known the weather was getting ugly and I would have called Aggie or driven over there. I could have found the kids before they . . . " She clamped her hand over her mouth.

Peggy could feel the pain that was growing inside the other woman. "I wish I could help," she said. "I can say that I know how you feel, because I do, but I also know that you don't need someone to understand. You need someone to take away the anguish."

"Yes," Janet said, looking around at the girl.

"It was like this the night Tom died," Peggy said. She hadn't been able to talk about it for a long time. People didn't want to listen. It made them squirm uncomfortably. So she didn't talk about it.

But for some reason she knew she could talk to Janet Cord. "It was snowing and we could hardly drive that night, but we were in a hurry to get to my folks' home. We should have stopped at a motel. Tom wanted to. But I thought I could handle the storm. So he let me drive. I didn't see the truck until it was too late. Tom died in the hospital. That was last spring."

Janet was silent, sensing how badly Peggy needed to get it all out.

Peggy looked up at the portrait of Christ that hung over the fireplace. This family believed in God, she was sure of that. It wasn't just that picture. It was the Bibles and the records and the plaques in the kitchen too. What if they didn't find their children alive? Would they turn bitter against God? Or would their faith be strong enough to endure it?

She looked at Janet again. Here was a woman who wouldn't give out pat answers. She knew the agony. If she said anything it would be real. "We were on our way to Bolivia," Peggy said. "We were going to be missionaries. We were so excited and happy. We had finished our training. We had our shots and our passports and our money."

"Oh Peggy!" Janet cried.

"I've never been able to understand. Tom would have given his whole life to God. The world needs men like him. Why did God take him? Why didn't He take somebody who—who doesn't deserve to live? It doesn't make sense."

Janet put her arms around the younger woman. Her own emotions and doubts and questions clogged up the words in her throat. She didn't understand any more than Peggy did. What could she say?

Late in the afternoon, Janet saw her husband and the deputy ride into the yard. Fear and hope clutched at her stomach. She ran across the room and flung open the door. Her eyes swept Cord's face, and she knew without asking that they had not found Brian and Krissie. She stepped aside and let them enter the house. They looked exhausted. Their eyebrows were white and their faces were red and wind-whipped and splotched with white. Frostbite. She knelt down and helped Cord with his boots.

"We had to quit," Cord said. The lower part of his face refused to function, causing his words to slur thickly. "We couldn't see. We kept going in circles. If we hadn't smacked into the fence we might never have gotten out." His voice was broken with grief.

He thinks they're dead! she thought. He's given up! She stifled the cry in her throat.

Rettick saw her thoughts and cursed silently, angry at his own helplessness. If only the two Brenner boys would have been able to make it to the outside and let someone know they needed help. Even if they had, how soon would it be before help could get through to them? And maybe it was already too late.

Peggy examined the men's hands and feet carefully. "Not too bad," she said. "All you need is some warm water to thaw them in. Do you have some basins or something like that, Jan?"

"How about if I just get close to the fire," Cord said.

Peggy shook her head firmly. "You want to get warm and you want to get warm fast, but not by using extreme heat. If there's any tissue damage, that will make it worse."

"She's a nurse," Jan said.

"Hey, that's great!" Cord said with enthusiasm. "I mean, if you're going to get trapped in a world of your own you might as well have a nurse along."

Janet looked at her husband. He was faking it. He was trying to cover up for her. In that moment she loved him more than she had ever loved him. A great longing came over her for her man. She wanted to reach out to him, to touch him, to hold him, to comfort him. But she couldn't.

She went to the utility room and found an old washtub. "How is this?"

"That's perfect," Peggy said, "as long as they don't mind sticking their feet in it together."

Janet poured the hot water into the tub while Peggy added snow until it was lukewarm. Janet brought several towels from the bathroom.

Michael stood close to her, watching the tall stranger who had come in with his father. "Is he a real cop?" he asked.

"Why don't you ask him?"

"Are you a real cop?" Michael asked. "Is that a real gun?"

Rettick eased his feet into the water. "I'm a deputy sheriff and this is a real gun." He grinned at the child.

Michael edged closer to Rettick. "Do you shoot bad guys?"

"I try not to shoot anybody," Rettick told him.

"Why? If I was a sheriff I'd shoot all the bad guys."

"He watches too much TV," Janet said, embarrassed.

"Most kids do these days." He felt the pack of cigarettes in his pocket. He had been craving a smoke all day. He glanced around the room. It was obvious these people didn't smoke.

"Do you have a police car?" Michael asked. He was standing next to Rettick now.

"Sometimes I use one, but right now I'm using my jeep."

"Oh," he said, disappointed.

"It has a siren though," Rettick said. "And a radio too."

"Can I ride in it?" He reached up and fingered the badge on Rettick's shirt.

"Michael," Cord said, "stop being a pest."

"He's not being a pest," Rettick said. He lifted the boy onto his lap. "Maybe tomorrow I can give you a ride."

"Oh boy! Wait until Brian and Krissie come home! They won't believe it!"

Nobody said anything for a long moment.

"Do you have some kids?" Michael asked.

"I have two. A boy and a girl. But they're older than you. The boy is almost ten and the girl is eleven."

"I bet your wife is worried sick about you," Janet said softly.

"No. She's not." He said it abruptly, coldly.

Janet gave him a surprised look. Was he divorced? Divorce was so tragic, especially when there were children involved.

Rettick reached for his cigarettes. He needed

one badly. "Do you mind if I smoke?" he asked her.

"No. Go ahead." She got up and brought him an ashtray she kept in the cupboard.

Michael watched him light up with fascination. "He's smoking a stick, Mommy." He watched the end glow. "My mommy said smoking makes you get cancer."

Janet tried to shush him.

Rettick chuckled. "You're a smart kid," he said. "Your mommy is right. Smoking does give you cancer. That's one reason you should never do it."

"How come you do then?"

"Because when I was a little boy I thought it would be fun to smoke. And then, after awhile I couldn't stop smoking."

"How come?"

"That's what happens. Have you ever had a little piece of chocolate from a candy bar?"

"Yeah."

"What happened when you ate it? Did you want more or was that enough?"

"I wanted more."

"That's how it is with smoking."

"Does it taste good?"

"Not really. But you still can't quit."

"I'm about half-starved," Cord said. "You know what would taste good? Some hot stew. You still have plenty of that roast left, don't you?"

"Yes," Janet said.

"Couldn't you use that?"

"I used all the broth for gravy."

"I'd settle for soup then."

Janet went to the kitchen. "What kind?"

"Anything. How about you?" he asked Rettick.

"I'm not fussy."

Janet placed two cans of Campbell's Chunky chicken and noodle soup on the counter. She tried to open them. No electricity. She hunted through the drawers for an old hand-operated can opener.

She went to the kitchen door. "I can't open the cans. I need electricity."

"We don't have one of the other kind of can openers?"

"I can't find one."

"Well don't we have some of that soup that comes in the packages? Lipton's or whatever?"

"No." She snapped her fingers. "I have bouillon! I could make stew with that!"

Peggy came into the kitchen. "Can I help?"

"Sure. I'll use frozen vegetables. That way it won't take so long. Throw anything in that looks good." She cut the roast into small chunks, added onion, stirred in the bouillon and seasoned it. Peggy dumped a package of frozen mixed vegetables in with the other food.

"Should I cook some potatoes?" Janet asked.

"This looks good to me." She thickened the broth, stirring it constantly. They ladled it into stoneware bowls.

"What do you do for a living?" Rettick asked Cord as they ate.

"I'm an electrical contractor."

"It's a good trade. Brings in good money, I hear."

"If you're lucky."

"All I know is you guys charge through the nose for your work."

"I wish you could see my books."

Rettick finished his stew and lit a cigarette. "I guess it's the old story: everybody thinks the other guy is giving him the short end of the stick." He leaned forward. "Say! You own Cord Electric, don't you?"

"That's right."

"I remember reading about you in connection with that Jennings Construction swindle. I was on that case."

"Anything new on Jennings?"

Rettick shook his head. "Nothing. We're sure he skipped the country. Or he's living somewhere else under a new identity. You lost a couple thousand dollars on him, didn't you?"

"Ten."

"Ten thousand?" Rettick whistled softly. "I bet that put a hole in your pocket."

"Yep. I lost my shirt."

Rettick shook his head. Why did it always happen to the nice guys like Cord? He and his wife were getting put through the ringer lately, and it didn't seem right. They were friendly, honest people, basically good. Rettick had a habit of analyzing people's faces and filing them away in his mind. He never forgot a face. Most of the time he could tell what a person was by studying his face. Jim and Jan Cord had good, open faces.

He shifted his gaze toward Peggy Caldwell. She was pretty. Naturally so. Striking in fact. But something or someone had hurt her badly. Her face was taut with the hurt, and with bitterness too.

The hours plodded away through the evening. Michael changed into his pajamas and climbed onto his father's lap and went to sleep. Janet sat next to them, staring into the fire. Peggy sat with a book in her hand, not reading.

Rettick smoked steadily, nervously, the way he always did when he had nothing else to do. He cursed the radio in his jeep, the phones, the avalanche, the blizzard, his complete and utter helplessness.

He thought briefly of Valerie, his wife. Would she be gone when he got home? Had they called and told her he was missing? Would she care? For some reason he couldn't comprehend, he wished she would care.

He shrugged away those thoughts and the memories of happy years when they had loved instead of fought. People were so sure they controlled their lives, so sure they could plan out how it would be for them. But sooner or later they had to realize there was a Force in existence that they couldn't control—a Force that could create havoc with their carefully planned lives.

Rettick looked at the Cords. It was obvious from things they had around the house that they were religious—probably very religious. He had seen all kinds of religious people with varying degrees of dedication to their beliefs. Some of them made it through times of crisis by clinging to their faith, some of them didn't. He hoped the Cords would.

On the couch by the fire, Janet stirred, and then she got up. She walked to the window and stood looking out. The sky was pallid and whitewashed. The wind moaned in the trees, and wailed over the flats. The fenceposts formed a cadaverous, eerie row of mounds. Janet stood there for a long time, looking out, watching the storm through the darkness, thinking of nothing.

Suddenly she felt a hard lump of anger clotting her chest. She turned toward the others. "Why is God doing this to us? Why is He hurting us this way?"

They looked up at her, startled.

Her question shot straight into Cord's brain and sank like a cold rock to the bottom of his subconscious, stirring his own questions and doubt. He felt black, ugly despair surge through him.

He got up from the couch, still holding Michael, and stood in front of the fire, watching it crackle and sputter and roar over the charred logs.

A man couldn't live this way, half-believing God. There was no such thing as half trust. Either you believed or you didn't. It was all or nothing.

He wondered exactly what it was that he didn't believe about God.

If he believed the basic premise, that God loved him, Jim Cord, so much that He had put his life above the life of His only Son—if he believed that, then he had to believe that God would take the best possible care of his life, a life which had cost Him everything. It wasn't logical or realistic to believe the first and not the second.

Didn't he believe then that God was as powerful as He claimed to be? Didn't he believe that God was in full control, that the entire universe was in His hands? Of course he believed those things because he believed that God was the Creator of everything in existence.

So why was he questioning God?

Suddenly Cord knew how it had to be for him. He laid Michael down and went to his wife. "It's not enough to believe the facts of Christianity," he said quietly. "It's not even enough to accept Jesus Christ into your life. It's much, much more than that."

"What are you talking about?" she asked.

"I'm talking about us, Jan. About the way we believe in God. About the doubts we've both had, and the anger, toward God." He had forgotten the others in the room, and he spoke carefully, measuring and weighing his words and his thoughts.

"Believing in God—I mean really believing in God—is handing over your life, yourself, your family, your work, everything you are, everything you hope to be, everything you have. It's handing it over totally to a Living Personal God, and saying to Him: I'm Yours; You use me and whatever I possess in whatever way You wish; You fill Your needs with my life."

He took Jan's face between his hands gently. "And then, you don't take it back. No matter what happens, no matter how much you don't understand, no matter how badly you hurt, you keep trusting Him. You trust Him because of what you know He is and because of what you know He has done for you already just by giving His life for you." He was speaking to himself more than to her. His hands tightened on her face. "It's trusting Him even if . . . " He paused, his voice broken. "Even if He takes everything. Even the kids."

"Oh Jim!" The tears she hadn't been able to shed before were torn from her in great gulping sobs.

Rettick and Peggy looked at each other, then got up from their chairs and went to their rooms, leaving the Cords alone with their grief.

After a long time, Cord and his wife stirred from their embrace. "Let's go to bed," he said, "and try to get some sleep. We're going to need our strength to face whatever lies ahead."

Janet nodded. She was exhausted, drained, empty. She lifted Michael from the couch and followed her husband to the bedroom.

They laid Michael in the bed and then climbed in beside him without undressing. Janet lay with her back against Cord, and he spooned her body with his own.

"Jim?"

"Yes?"

"Does it hurt to freeze to death?"

"I don't know."

"Maybe you just lose the feeling in your body and then go to sleep."

"Maybe." He had read about some young boys who had gotten lost in the Alps, caught in a blizzard. When they found the boys, buried in the snow, their faces had been frozen into grimaces of terrible pain. But maybe that was merely the freezing process deforming their faces. Maybe it hadn't really been pain at all. "No," he said decisively. "It doesn't hurt."

"I'm glad."

The house became quiet except for the snapping and popping of the fire in the living room and the moaning of the wind outside, and the sound of Michael's soft snoring. Janet reached out and drew her youngest son against her, needing to feel the life in his body, and Cord lay his arm over them both. Finally, they slept.

In Brian's room, Mitch Rettick lay awake, staring into the blackness. He was alone in the room, and yet, he had the feeling that he wasn't alone at all, that another Presence was there with him, and that he was being irresistibly drawn toward that Presence.

A crazy blinding fear fell on him. If he didn't resist, the Presence would swallow and absorb and annihilate him. He broke out into a cold sweat.

Run!
Run!
Run!

The feeling left him. He stretched out his tense body in the bed. What was with him? He was like a kid waking from a nightmare, sweating and panting and full of terror. He groped in the darkness for a cigarette and a match.

He had never been much on religion. When he was a kid, his parents sent him to Sunday School. He never could figure out why, because they didn't believe in God, but he had had fun there, and he liked the stories, so he never asked.

Then, when he was nine years old, he had a teacher who told them about Hell.

Hell, she said, was a place you'd have to go to after you died if you didn't believe in Jesus—if you didn't belong to Him.

It was a place of terrible pain, worse than you could ever imagine, and it lasted forever and ever and it never once stopped hurting.

Not only that, but you couldn't be with the people you loved when you were in Hell. You got taken away from them and sometimes you could see them from far off, but you could never, ever talk to them or be with them.

And there was still more. Hell was a place where you never got to have anything you wanted, and you never got to do anything you wanted. Everything that was important to you was taken away.

In Hell there could never be any love or hope or happiness. Only hate and sadness and pain and every other bad thing you could imagine.

He had sat there listening to those simplified words, that horrible appalling description of Hell, and he had been terrified.

Later, he had said, "I hate God."

"Why?" his teacher had asked.

"Because He makes people go to Hell."

The teacher had led him gently to a chair and sat down with him. "Mitch," she had said, "God doesn't make anyone go there. People only go there because they don't want to belong to Him. They don't want anything to do with Him. Do you think they'd be happy in Heaven with God around close to them all the time when they didn't want Him near them at all? They'd hate it."

"Why can't they just stay here?"

"Because God has to punish people for turning against Him and for breaking His laws. He doesn't want to hurt anyone. That's why He sent His only Son, Jesus, to take the punishment for us. But if people won't accept Jesus, then He has to punish them."

"Then I hate Him."

"You should love Him, Mitch. He loves you very much."

But he had been angry and he had turned away, and after that he had never wanted to go to Sunday School again.

Rettick smoked carefully in the bed, remembering. His next encounter with God had been equally as bad. He and Valerie had already been married several years, and they were happy and in love. She had been wonderful then, exciting and full of life and wildness.

Then she had met Karen, a quiet sort of woman who lived at the other end of the block, and she and Karen had become close friends.

One night he had come home and found her waiting up for him. She had been almost quivering with some kind of excitement and joy that he didn't understand. She told him she had accepted Christ into her life and into her being and she tried to explain what it meant.

He still didn't understand. All he knew was that she had changed, and he had been consumed by the fear that he was going to lose her.

She began to change. She was always studying her Bible and going to church and visiting friends who did the same. She kept begging him to go with her. Her talk was filled with things she was learning about God and man.

She told him how only a Superior Being could have masterminded the creation of the universe. It could never have merely happened by chance and been so perfectly balanced, so intricately formed even to the most minute detail. Nothing but a Superior Being could have created life.

He told her he believed that as much as she did. So what was the big deal?

Then she told him how this Being was God and

how He possessed emotions. That He'd had such a need to love and to be loved that He'd created for Himself other beings very much like Himself—human beings who could fulfill His needs.

She told him that even as He had created them, He had known He would have to give them the freedom to choose or not to choose Him because love can be neither bought nor forced. And that He had known from the beginning that they would turn away from Him and that they would become alienated from Him so completely that there would never be any hope of their ever returning to Him.

And still, He had been so consumed by His need for them that He had made a Plan that would make it possible for them to come to Him if they wanted Him after all. And this Plan was that He Himself would one day come to them as one of them and completely identify with them and that in the end He would give His own Life for them.

It had reminded Rettick of Sunday School and the story of Hell. He had laughed at his wife and told her she sounded like a silly child believing in fairy tales. He had said to her, "If God died, then He's dead. What good does that do you?"

"It was His Son, Jesus, who died."

"And you believe Jesus was God, right?"

"Yes. God has three parts: God the Father, God the Son and then His Spirit. It's like an apple. An apple has the peel, the meat, and the core. All three parts make one apple, not three separate apples. That's how God is. And because He loved us,

He sent a part of Himself to die—to take the punishment for our wrongdoing. It was the only way He could get us back. And then He put new life back into His Son so that His Son could put new life into us. And when we have faith enough to choose Him, then He puts His Spirit within us."

He had snorted with disgust at her and walked out. Two weeks later he told her they were moving away, and after they moved he ordered her to stay away from church and he threw her Bible in the fire.

She had never been the same after that. He thought that after awhile she would return to her old ways and they would be happy again, but he was wrong.

A year later, he saw posters announcing a special singing group. They believed the Bible, the poster read, and they preached the Bible. He mentioned it to Valerie.

"You can go if you'd like. And I'll go with you." Anything was better than the way things were then. But Valerie simply wasn't interested. She didn't care. He had killed a part of her. It was too late.

Sometime in the middle of the night, Cord was awakened suddenly. Something was wrong. He sat up in the bed, straining his ears to hear a sound, but there was nothing. The night was as still and silent as death.

Then he knew. There was no wind. He leaped from the bed and tore open the curtains.

Janet jerked awake, filled with fright. "What is it? What's the matter?"

"It's over," he said. "The storm is over."

They stood together at the window, looking outside. The sky was studded with a million frozen stars and moonlight poured softly over the snow-draped trees and earth.

"Isn't it beautiful?" Jan whispered.

"The most beautiful thing I've ever seen," he answered. They lay in bed and waited for the new day.

11

Morning broke in the eastern sky over the rim of the mountains, dazzling the snow-smothered earth with the white-gold blaze of the sun.

Cord, Brenner and the two boys listened quietly as the deputy outlined the plan he had put together during breakfast.

"You two boys are sure you can make it through to the outside today?" he asked.

"Yeah. Sure. The only reason we couldn't make it yesterday was that we couldn't see worth a hoot and we got chicken. I mean, that hill is steep! You want to know what's coming up next."

"We need Search and Rescue. We won't wait around for them, but we need them here as soon as possible. If they can't do anything else, they could get an ambulance and have it waiting on the other side of the avalanche."

The boys nodded eagerly.

"Another thing you can do is try to recruit help

from the ranchers in the area. Men with snowmobiles. We need all the manpower we can get."

"There are homes all through this canyon," Cord said. "And most people own at least one snowmobile."

Rettick nodded. "I thought the three of us could organize a search party with volunteers in the area. We also need to find out if anyone saw the kids on Saturday afternoon. We've been assuming those kids went directly to and from the hill on Brenner's property, and we've confined our search to that area. But we can't be certain the kids even went to that hill. Kids are unpredictable. Even the best behaved don't always obey or follow their normal behavior patterns. We have to cover every possibility. Was there tension and conflict at home that day? If so, did the kids run away and eventually get lost? Or did they take the road and get picked up by a stranger? Or did they simply decide to go somewhere else to use their sleds? Boys especially are always looking for something bigger and better, and maybe your boy saw a hill one day that looked as if it would be more fun."

Cord rubbed his chin thoughtfully. "I see what you mean. Even if the kids did go to that hill on Brenner's property, they might have been having so much fun that the storm caught them by surprise. They could have lost all sense of direction."

"Exactly. So we've got to move out. Cover more ground. There's a chance those kids are still alive. Let's get to them."

"If we get help," Kevin asked, "how will we find you?"

"That's one thing I haven't figured out yet," Rettick said.

"Couldn't we just follow your tracks?" Randy asked. "There sure wouldn't be any other tracks around today."

Rettick grinned sheepishly. "I guess that's as good a way as any. We might as well leave, then."

Cord reached out to his wife. He saw the calm in her eyes, felt the new strength in her body as he held her against him, and he drew from her as she had drawn from him last night. She knew now, as he did, that they might not find Brian and Krissie alive, but he was certain that she would be okay. He had felt her shoulders jerking with silent sobs off and on during the night when she had thought he was asleep, and he had heard the faint movement of her lips in prayer.

She touched his face gently at first, then slid her arms around his neck and hugged him fiercely. She was trembling and her eyes were wet, but she was still calm deep inside herself. They said nothing to each other.

Cord and Rettick went to the garage for the snowmobiles. Cord rolled the heavy door over their heads and started up his machine. He took it outside, waited for Rettick, and reached up to pull the door down into place.

His eyes caught sight of a sled propped against the wall. He hadn't noticed it before. He read the name that had been carefully spelled out across the top of it with a thick red marking pen: KRISSIE CORD.

"Krissie's sled!" he shouted at the others. He burst across the snow and into the house. "Jan! Jan!"

She was still standing by the door where he had left her, and she stepped back in startled surprise.

He grabbed her arm. "Krissie's sled is in the garage."

She stared.

Rettick and Brenner entered the house.

"You said they went sledding. Right?"

"Yes."

"Tell me exactly what happened."

She was flustered. "Uh... I told Brian to shovel the walks for you. He was in his room. He was very upset about something. Uh... at the table, when you went to answer the phone, I asked him if he was still mad at you..." She paused, remembering the others.

"Go on," Cord urged. "You mean about the night before when I let him have it."

She nodded. "He said he wasn't, but I think he was. He hardly ate anything. And then he ran off to his room. I think he was crying in there. He wouldn't come out when I called him."

"So anyhow, you told him to shovel the walks."

"Right. After awhile he sneaked outside and did them. The next thing I knew, he was in here getting all dressed up in his long underwear and stuff and he and Krissie were fighting because she wanted to go with him and he wouldn't let her. I said he had to take her."

"And he said he was going to Richie's to go sledding?"

"Yes, I think so." She thought back to that day. "Yes. That's why I made him take Krissie. Because the last time he went, he fussed and fussed about taking her and I told him he could go without her if he promised to take her the next time. Oh, Jim, you don't think he would have run off without her, do you? And she followed him?"

"No. If she'd have followed him she would have taken her sled. More than likely she would have come crying to you."

"That's true."

"I don't understand why they didn't take her sled," Cord said. "Unless... unless Brian figured it would be easier and quicker to pull her on his toboggan." He looked at Rettick for help. "What do you think?"

"If the toboggan is gone it seems logical that that's what they did," Rettick said. "They may have tried the sled and given up on it. It's hard to pull a sled in deep snow."

The others agreed. So there was nothing new after all.

Janet pressed her forehead against the cold window and watched them leave. She had seen the expression of guilt and pain come into her husband's face when she had mentioned his anger with Brian the night before. Oh Jim...

She had felt him willing his strength and courage into her last night, and this morning, drawing it back into himself. He was afraid, he was guiltridden, he was hurting more than he had ever hurt in his life, but he was also strong with his new trust in God. She had the same split in herself—the trust and calm and the fear.

Her mind settled on Brian as he had been on Saturday. Why hadn't she gone into his room to talk things out the way she usually did? Michael was sick, of course, and she had been preoccupied with losing the house.

Stupid house. How important was it now in comparison with her children's lives? It was so trivial. Funny how very trivial it really seemed to her now when it had been such a big thing Saturday.

Peggy came and stood beside her. "It's beautiful, isn't it."

Janet looked through the window. "Krissie would say it looks like whipped cream," she said.

Peggy touched her arm softly. "Are you okay?"

Janet nodded.

"I wish I could do something," Peggy said helplessly.

Janet turned and looked directly into her face. "I'm okay. I really am okay."

She was. Peggy could sense the calm in her, and she knew it had nothing to do with either shock or with an unrealistic false hope. She had come to terms with the worst and she had accepted it—not fatalistically, but with the confidence that God loved her and her children and that if He had to allow them to be hurt this deeply it was only for a very good reason.

Peggy knew this without needing to be told, and a part of her own self cried out for release from the bitterness that had woven itself into every fiber of her being.

"It's like Jim told me last night: either you trust God or you don't. You can't believe He'd give up everything He had for you and then believe He'd deliberately set out to hurt you."

But He does, Peggy said silently.

"I don't understand this," Janet continued. "It would be so much easier if I could understand. All I know is that I have to trust Him. You know, it's one thing to say you trust Him. It's another thing to follow Him through the darkness."

Peggy closed her eyes and remembered her nightmare. She had trusted. She had followed through the darkness. She had fallen and fallen and fallen into emptiness. God had betrayed her.

"Right now," Janet said, "I feel as if my whole world is falling apart around me. I feel as if I'm dying, inch by inch. And yet, at the same time, I can feel God's love holding me up."

Peggy listened numbly. She had to get away from here, to be alone. "It's so pretty outside," she managed to say. "I think I'd like to go for a walk."

Janet simply nodded.

Peggy slipped into her winter clothes and stepped outside. The clean, cold air pierced her lungs. She jammed her hands deep into her pockets and walked away from the house.

Her mind played out her life and her dreams, and her sorrow, her guilt, her bitterness broke over her for a moment, until she wept.

Why did You take him, God?

She remembered something Tom had said once, before they were married. He had come to her all excited over something he had discovered in the Bible.

"It says right here that we were created by Him for His own pleasure. Most of us live as if He had been created for our pleasure."

It had meant nothing to her.

"Don't you see?" he had cried. "It's our reason for existing! Our purpose for living is to live for God. To please God. It makes everything fall into place!"

She had loved his exuberance even though she hadn't fully shared it, or understood it.

She understood now. Jim Cord had seen it last night. What had he said? Oh yes, I'm Yours. You use me in whatever way You wish: You fill Your needs with my Life. And his understanding of the way it should be, and his acceptance of that, had renewed his faith in God and strengthened him for whatever lay ahead.

Oh help me, please help me, she prayed. She stood in the frozen sunlight, hardly feeling the cold that gnawed at her under the quilted lining of her coat. She looked back at the house and saw Janet Cord framed in the window of the living room with her youngest child in her arms.

She had Roddie. He was still a baby, but she needed to begin teaching him to love God the way his father had. And later, well, later, when Roddie was older, maybe she would make it to Bolivia. Or somewhere else.

But for now, Roddie was enough. She would find her way back to God, and they would grow together, she and Roddie, and God would be there with them.

As Peggy walked slowly to the house where Jan waited, Cord, Brenner and the deputy sheriff pulled alongside the high chain-link fence that surrounded Chuck and Lynda Bobocel's place. The dogs, still chained-up in the back, began to raise a ruckus.

"I have my doubts about this place," Cord said. "The kids would have been scared to death of those dogs."

"We still need Bobocel's help," Brenner said. "I know he's got two snowmobiles."

"He's also got dogs," the deputy said quietly.

The others stared.

"We've used his dogs before," Rettick said. "We used them to find a little girl just last summer."

"I remember!" Brenner said. "They found her body in the. . . ." He broke off, thinking of Cord.

"In the river," Cord finished. "I remember too, although I didn't realize they were Chuck Bobocel's dogs."

"They're good dogs," Rettick said. "I know

there wouldn't be any trail to follow, but I'm sure they could ferret the kids out."

"You mean if they're buried under a drift."

"Yes."

Bobocel stepped out of the house, bellowing at the dogs. He shielded his eyes against the sun-bright snow to see his visitors. "Can I help you?"

"I'm Deputy Sherriff Mitch Rettick." He opened the gate, approaching the man on the porch.

"Something wrong?" Bobocel asked. He shifted a wad of tobacco to the other side of his lip and spat into the snow. He was young—in his early twenties, Rettick guessed—with a long, sinewy sun-bronzed body and sharp blue eyes. He wore faded jeans and a t-shirt, and he hung his thumbs on his back pockets and waited for the deputy.

"There's two kids missing. Got lost in the blizzard Saturday afternoon. The avalanche—there's been an avalance on the other side of the fork—has us penned in here. We're scrounging up a search party. Men with snowmobiles."

Bobocel nodded. "I'll be with you right away."

"Can the dogs be of any help?"

"We can try them. Do you have any idea where the kids went?"

"We think so."

Bobocel looked past Rettick at the men outside the gate. "Do you expect to find them alive?"

"I don't think so. I don't know. Maybe they got lucky. They're little. Five and eight."

Bobocel shook his head. "Whose kids are they?"

"Jim Cord's. They live in the first house in the canyon."

Lynda Bobocel came to the door. "What's going on?" She saw the deputy. "Has something happened?"

"Some kids got lost," her husband said. "They need help." He went inside to get dressed.

"Why don't you all come in and wait?" Lynda invited.

"We've got to be going. Those kids have been out there since Saturday. You didn't happen to see two little kids Saturday afternoon, did you? A boy and girl. They had a dog with them."

Lynda felt a chill creep over her. "What are their names?"

"Uh, Brian and Kristine or something. They belong to Jim Cord."

"They were here," she said in a low voice.

"We're going ahead," Cord shouted at Rettick. "We'll meet you at the last house."

"You said those kids were here?" Rettick repeated.

"Yes."

"Wait a minute!" Rettick shouted. "Cord! Wait a minute!"

Cord and Brenner shut off their machines. "What's up?"

Rettick turned back to Bobocel's wife. "When were they here?"

"Saturday afternoon."

"You're sure? They're just little kids."

"Yes."

Rettick motioned the other men to come into the yard. "She says the kids were here."

"Are you sure?" Cord asked.

She nodded. "Brian and Krissie and their dog. They shoveled the walks for me."

Bobocel came outside. "What's this?"

"You remember I told you there were two little kids here on Saturday? I let them shovel the walks."

He nodded. "The boy you were so impressed with."

"Wait a minute," Cord said. "You said they shoveled your walks?"

"They wanted to earn some money. They had two shovels. Brian was pulling Krissie on a toboggan. I didn't need to have it done, but the kid nearly cried when I said no. He said he needed. . . ." She paused, wondering if she should tell him. "You have one terrific little boy, Mr. Cord."

"He wanted a snowmobile. I didn't know how badly. I don't suppose he understands how much they cost."

"No," Lynda said, "it wasn't for a snowmobile. It was for you. He said you needed money and he wanted to help. He even asked if I'd let him work around here this summer."

Cord stood stock still. Brian, outside the kitchen door, his face filled with an unreadable expression. Brian, upset at the table, not eating, not wanting to play. Brian, planning to earn some money, being forced to drag his little sister along. Brian had heard them talking, fighting, in the kitchen Saturday morning. He had stood outside the door listening and he had heard how his dad was flat broke. And he had tried to help. Oh, God, what have I done?

"Where did they go from here?" he asked huskily.

"I made them come in to warm up and eat a snack. And then they headed up the road to the next house. They were so exhausted. I wanted them to go home. But he insisted he had to get some more jobs."

"All this time we've been searching the wrong area," Cord said. "They never went to Brenners' at all. It was all a cover-up so Jan wouldn't know what they were really up to. I don't suppose they got caught in the storm and someone took them in. I mean, by this time they'd have brought them home."

It came to him clearly then. "They would have taken the shortcut home. I'm sure of it!"

"This is a different shortcut than the one we searched earlier?" Rettick asked.

Cord nodded. "Richie and Brian use it all the time when they go fishing. Mrs. Bobocel, can I borrow a piece of paper and a pencil, please?"

"Sure. Come on in."

They stood around the kitchen table while

Cord drew a rough map. "Between our house and the last house in the canyon is about a three-mile stretch of road. Uphill all the way. Brian would have taken any shortcut he could find. Now, between our house and the last house there is actually only about a quarter of a mile of heavily wooded area if you cut straight across instead of taking the road. If I remember correctly, there is sort of a faded-out jeep trail to follow. But of course it would have been covered with snow."

"And where is Brenners'?" Rettick asked.

Cord drew the Snow Mountain Ski Resort road. "His ranch lies between the two roads. The kids would have cut through the area on the other side of Rock Creek Canyon Road."

Brenner snapped his fingers. "Don't Brian and Richie have some kind of hideout around there?"

"I don't recall hearing Brian talk about one."

"Seems like Richie has mentioned it a few times. It was a secret. He wouldn't say anything except that they had one."

"It could be anything," Rettick said. "In or under a tree. A hole in the rocks. Some kind of lean-to they built. It's hard to tell. Boys are imaginative at that age. I remember my kid."

"Why don't I chug on home and ask Richie?" Brenner suggested.

"I hate to waste the time," Cord said. "We don't even know they're there. They could have wandered around and got lost."

"Brenner can go home," Rettick said. "We'll

see if we can round up some more men. You should be able to find us easily enough. We won't be moving fast."

They heard the whine of snowmobiles outside, and the dogs barking in the back.

Cord looked through the window. "It's the neighbors from down the road."

"Good," Rettick said. "Let's get the show on the road."

"I'm coming along," Lynda said. She stood in the doorway, zipped up in a bright blue snowmobile suit.

The men exchanged glances.

"It's okay," Bobocel said. "She's used to it. She goes out with me all the time. She can help with the dogs. We need all the help we can get."

"I feel partly to blame," Lynda said.

"Don't blame yourself," Cord said firmly. "There's no point in it. If anyone's to blame it's me, not you."

"You don't mind if I go along, do you?" she asked.

Cord smiled. "I don't mind at all," he said. "I just thank God you came to the door. We'd have spent another day searching the wrong area if you hadn't."

Bobocel grunted, moving toward the door. As far as he was concerned, God was a crutch for those who couldn't make it on their own. Everything he had, he'd gotten with his own two bare hands and his brain. He didn't need God or anybody else to help him through his life. People invented God. They conjured Him up to fit their needs and desires. He wondered if Cord was one of these religious nuts who claimed God talked to them. It was hard for him to believe anyone in a civilized country could believe it was anything other than communicating with one's own subconscious. Well, to each his own. He spat on the ground and went to the kennels to get his dogs.

"We'll need some of Krissie and Brian's clothing for the dogs," Rettick said.

"I could pick it up when I go home," Brenner offered.

"It'd probably be faster if I take the shortcut," Cord said. "We'll need those clothes right away." He waved and ran his machine across the road and into the wooded area that lay in the three-mile loop.

Brenner headed back toward his house.

"What's going on?" Aggie asked as he walked in.

"I need Richie. Where is he?"

"He just went outside to play."

"Back yard?"

"Yes."

Brenner strode swiftly to the back door. "Richie! Come in here for a minute."

"Did they find Brian and Krissie?" Richie asked.

"No. Not yet." He looked down at his skinny red-haired kid. "Richie, we need your help. We just found out that Brian and Krissie never came here at all on Saturday."

"They didn't?" Aggie asked. "So you were looking in all the wrong places?"

"Yes. Brian and Krissie were trying to earn money by shoveling walks."

"Hey, that's a great idea!"

"Just listen to me, Richie. We're pretty sure they took the shortcut—you know, the one between the last house in the lower canyon and Cords' house."

"Yeah. We take it all the time when we go fishing."

"Okay. Now I remember hearing you mention a fort or a hideout that you and Brian have around there someplace."

Richie's mind went immediately to the old abandoned house. The first time he and Brian had found it, he had told his mom about it and she had been really mad—especially about the part where they climbed down the root cellar. She told him to stay away from the place. It was too dangerous and they might get hurt.

"Richie?" his dad said.

Richie shuffled his feet and looked at the floor. He didn't know what to do. He would really be in big trouble from his mom if he told about the house, and besides, there was that oath he and Brian had taken when they became blood brothers that they would never tell, no matter what.

Brenner watched his son closely. What was

bugging him? Why wouldn't he tell? "Richie," he said irritably, "Brian and Krissie will die if we don't find them soon. You'd feel awfully bad if they were in your hideout and we couldn't find them, wouldn't you?"

He nodded, sliding his eyes sideways to look at this mother. Boy, was he going to get it! And Brian would be steaming mad at him for telling too. Or would he?

"Why won't you tell me?" his dad asked.

"We took an oath never to tell anybody."

"If you were lost and you finally got to the hideout but you couldn't make it home because you were too cold and tired and maybe hurt, would you want Brian to tell?"

"Yes," he said slowly. Because Brian would be the only one who would know where he was. He glanced at his mother, wishing she would leave the room. But she wouldn't, he knew, and besides, she would find out later from Dad.

"There's an old house," he said so quietly that Brenner had to lean down to hear him. "We always climb down into the root cellar. That's where we have our secret hideout."

Brenner felt excitement pour through him like a shot of adrenaline. "Can you tell me exactly where it is?"

"Is that the old house I told you never to play in again?" his mother asked.

Richie kept his head down.

"Richie!"

He nodded.

"You promised you'd never go back there. You're going to get a good spanking, young man."

Richie clenched his fists. Boy oh boy!

"Do you know where it is?" Brenner asked his wife.

"Somewhere behind Cords' house I think."

"It's past it on the other side," Richie said.

"What do you mean?"

"It's not in the shortcut. You go past Brian's house."

"How far past?"

"Pretty far."

"How in the world did you kids find it?" his mother asked.

"We were exploring."

"You have no business running around all over the woods," she said angrily. "And that house!"

"Aggie," Brenner said softly. "Leave it alone this time."

"Do you think they're there?" Richie asked.

"It would be a perfect place," Brenner said, "but it's too far out of the way. If it's so secret, Brian would never take Krissie there just for fun. He'd only take her there if he had to. But they wouldn't have been near that place on Saturday."

Richie's shoulders sagged. He should never have told. Now they knew and he was in trouble and it was all for nothing.

Brenner reached down and rumpled his son's hair. "Thanks for telling me," he said. "I know it spoiled everything. But if they had been there, you might have saved their lives. I'm sure Brian will understand."

Brenner left the house feeling flat with disappointment. They could always check out the old house, but there didn't seem to be much point in it. Poor Jim. Losing two of his kids. How was he going to get through it? Maybe his religion would hold him up. He never said much about it, but Brenner got the idea that he and Janet took their religious ideas quite seriously.

Brenner took the road wide open, hoping nobody was fool enough to try driving this morning. He came to the last house on the loop and found the snow behind it streaked with snowmobile tracks. He followed the muddle of lines through the trees.

"Brenner's back!" someone yelled.

The others gathered around him.

"Did you find anything out?" Cord asked.

Brenner shook his head regretfully. "They have a hideout, but it's way on the other side of your place."

He saw the hope die in Cord's eyes. "Sorry, buddy."

"It was a good try."

"Let's get back to work," Rettick said.

Cord, Brenner, the deputy, Chuck and Lynda Bobocel and five other volunteers from the canyon spread out through the tall, slender trees that stood like a million matchsticks end on end all over the flat and into the hills. The Bobocels separated, going to opposite ends of the search party, each taking two of the dogs.

The snow lay smooth and clean, without tracks or marks except those of small animals that had scurried away at the roaring of the snowmobiles that had destroyed the perfect quiet of the day.

The dogs pressed their noses into the soft snow and whimpered, finding no trace of the scent on the clothing. The storm had erased it all.

Suddenly Chuck's dogs leaped ahead, barking with excitement. They found a thick, well-protected brushy spot and scratched and pawed at the snow.

"Looks like they were here," Rettick said, pointing at the trampled spot. He stooped down and pulled a half-buried plastic bag from a piece of thorny brush. "Cookie crumbs?"

"That's the bag I gave them," Lynda said with excitement. "I sent some cookies along for them to snack on."

Brenner slammed his fist into his hand. "We're getting closer!"

The snowmobiles roared up again, combing the area with slow and painful precision. The sun slanted through the trees from the east, its blazing white light getting stronger as it climbed higher into the white-blue sky and flooding the snow with a resplendent glare.

Cord felt his anguish eating a hole through the middle of his gut. He rode reluctantly, as if by not finding the kids he could will them to be alive. His body ached and his eyes were tired, and he was soaked with sweat. As he maneuvered the heavy machine through the thick maze of brush and trees, a thin film of tears came across his eyes, blurring the snow-glazed world ahead of him, as if a shimmering translucent veil were softening the grim reality of the morning.

He could see himself striding through these same trees during the spring, when they were rustling with fresh green leaves in the warm breeze, and the earth was carpeted with tiny yellow and blue and pink wild flowers. And he was walking with his son, along the river bank, watching for a deep shaded pool where the big lunkers lay. And he was stretched out in the golden sunlight with a can of worms and his fishing pole, and his son was there beside him.

And they were having a picnic on a faded blanket in the grass. And he and Jan sat together with the baby between them, watching their daughter chase a butterfly through the trees, hearing her laughter float through the gentle air.

So long ago. When he had time for them and the business didn't swallow him with worry and frustration.

Oh my children . . .

I can't make it, God.

Then he remembered his promise of the night before and he soaked his fear-parched soul in God until he had absorbed strength enough to go on.

12

The sun was at the top of the sky, dazzling the trees and the earth, but not warming it. In a clearing near the Cords' home, the searchers stood beside their snowmobiles wondering what to do next. They were hungry and cold and tired, and their discouragement hung over them like a dark, heavy cloud.

"I don't know what to think," Bobocel said finally. "The dogs have come up with absolutely nothing since that spot in the brush. If the kids were here, I'm sure they'd find them."

"What if they're buried under a deep drift?" one of the neighbors asked in a low voice that he hoped Cord could not hear. "Would the dogs be able to smell them?"

"The drifts aren't that deep," Bobocel said.

"If only we had come here first," Brenner said. "We probably would have found them that night."

"They obviously came this way," Cord said. "They've got to be here."

"We've covered almost every square foot of ground within reasonable distance between the two houses," one of the men argued. "Maybe they headed off this way and the snow was too deep, so they cut back to the road."

"They could have done that," Rettick said, "but I don't think they would have. They were already quite a distance from the road when they stopped in the brush and ate their cookies."

"It's like they vanished into thin air," Lynda Bobocel said. "It's crazy."

"What if they did go to that old house?" Brenner asked.

"What old house?" Rettick questioned.

"The old house where Brian and my son have their hideout. It's somewhere beyond Cords' house. But the way it was blowing and snowing that night, they might have missed their house and kept on wandering until they stumbled onto the hideout."

"Why not?" Cord asked. Hope surged through his veins. "They sure aren't here."

"It's worth a try," Rettick said. "Do you know where it is?"

Brenner shook his head. "When my son told me it was way past Cords' house, I didn't bother to pinpoint the location."

"We can find it," someone said.

"I can go home and get Richie," Brenner said. "We're not far from my place now." He looked at Rettick.

Rettick paused, not knowing how to answer.

"It would save time," he said, "but . . . it might be hard for the boy."

Everyone's eyes went briefly to Cord.

"It's okay," he said quietly. "I'm fully aware of what we might find."

"If it helps us find the kids," Brenner said, "that's all that matters. I can take Richie away as soon as he shows us the house." He went to his snowmobile and reached for the ignition key, when suddenly they heard a sound in the distance.

"Helicopter!" Rettick shouted. "The boys got through! They got Search and Rescue!"

"Yahoo!" Brenner threw his hat into the air. "They'll be able to spot the old house from the air."

The helicopter came into sight, flying low over the trees. It came to Cords' house and circled several times, then rose higher for a better view of the area.

"Come on you guys," Rettick muttered. "Look down here."

The helicopter moved away from them toward Brenner's ranch.

Rettick cursed.

"The boys must have told them that's where we had been searching," Cord said quietly.

"I'll go ahead with our previous plan, then," Brenner said. "Maybe we'll get lucky and they'll see me. Or maybe they'll stop at the house and Aggie will tell them where we are." He started his machine and drove toward home.

"At least they're here now," Cord said, watching the helicopter move farther and farther away. "They'll spot us before too long. If . . . if the kids are still . . . alive . . . we'll need to get them to a hospital right away.

Rettick studied his face, marvelling at the calm he found in spite of the agony that had been etched into it. Yesterday he had been a man beaten with despair and the pain that was slowly killing him. Today he carried a new strength within him.

As a cop, he had seen men go to pieces under less pressure than Cord was under. But here was a man who honestly believed he should let God control and plan his life for him, and he believed it even when it seemed that God was allowing his whole life to fall apart. Last night, when he had talked to his wife, he sounded like a man who had found his reason for existing, a man fulfilled, a man at peace with himself and with his God.

Rettick shook his head. He didn't understand it, but whatever Cord had it was keeping him sane.

The searchers stomped their feet in the snow and rubbed their hands together, trying to keep warm.

"We could either build a fire or go on to my place while we wait for Brenner," Cord said.

"No," someone said. "He'll be back right away."

Nobody felt much like talking. Some of them thought of their own children, knowing the anguish they would be feeling now, and yet knowing that they couldn't even half imagine how terrible it would be.

Rettick reached inside his jacket for his cigarettes. He was out. Funny, he hadn't once thought about having a smoke since they had started the search early this morning.

"Need a cigarette?" one of the other men asked, offering his pack.

"Thanks." Rettick lit up, inhaling deeply. For some crazy reason he wanted to see his wife. He wanted her to be there when he got home. If only they could make it work between them.

They heard the buzz of Brenner's snowmobile, like the sound of a chainsaw in the distance. Then Brenner appeared through the trees with Richie on the long seat behind him. They started their machines, and Brenner motioned for them to follow him.

They fell into a long line, one behind the other, like a convoy, each filled with apprehension, wondering what they would find in the old abandoned house.

It stood before them in a small clearing by the frozen river, a colorless, broken sepulcher in the snow. They cut their engines, and the silence was deafening. Then the dogs went wild on their leashes.

"They're here," Bobocel said. He spat into the snow and ordered the dogs to be quiet.

"There's a trap door in the kitchen," Richie said. "Can I go down too?"

"No," his father said. "We're going home now."

"I want to see if Brian's there!"

Brenner shook his head. "If you need me again, let me know."

"Thanks," Rettick said. "You too, Richie." He waved as Brenner rode away. Then he entered the house.

Cord was already inside. He crawled over the debris from the ceiling and found the kitchen. He got down on his knees and peered into the open cellar. In the semi-darkness, he saw something.

"We need a flashlight!" Rettick yelled.

One of the men brought a flashlight. Rettick shined it into the hole. The dim yellow circle of light slid over the dirt floor to the dog and the tarp and the children beneath it.

"I'll go first," Cord said. As he descended into the cellar, he gathered himself together into a single prayer without words. His hands moved over Zane. The dog was cold and stiff, but he lifted his head and licked Cord's hand. "The dog's alive!" he called. He pulled the dog away from the children and lay aside the tarp. His hands trembled and he scarcely breathed as he touched his son's neck. He felt nothing. He yanked his gloves off and pressed his freezing fingers against the jugular vein and then to the side.

"I think I'm getting a pulse," he cried. He touched his fingers to Krissie's neck. "You try."

Rettick squatted beside him and groped for a pulse beat. "They're alive," he said. "Dog probably helped keep them warm."

"They're alive!" someone shouted above them. Outside, the dogs barked with excitement.

"Thank God," Cord whispered reverently. His throat was thick with emotion.

"Let's get them out of here!"

Cord and Rettick lifted the children gently, and carried them to the top. Lynda Bobocel brought the blankets and helped wrap them up carefully. They took them outside to the snowmobiles.

Rettick searched the sky briefly. "We'll take them home," he said. "We could use the rest of you to get that chopper for us so we can transport them to the hospital."

"I'll get the dog," one of the men said.

They left the old abandoned house as they had come, in a long line, one behind the other, but more slowly this time. It seemed to take years getting out of the forest. And then they were in the yard.

Janet came running across the snow to meet them.

Part Four

13

Rettick filled out a report on the shooting at Snow Mountain Ski Resort and one on the search for Brian and Krissie Cord.

The kids were in bad shape, the hospital had told him. He wondered how bad. He had been tempted to stay, but he had decided to go home instead. He could always call later and find out.

He felt the tension mounting within him, and he wondered if he should go home after all. What would he do if Valerie and the kids were gone? And what would he do if she were home?

"Need a ride?" one of the men asked.

Rettick looked up from the papers. "Yeah."

"You look like you need a month off. I guess it was pretty rough this weekend."

Rettick nodded. "Have they started clearing away the avalanche yet?"

"A few hours ago I think." As they got into the patrol car, the other deputy gave him a keen look. "Want to get a drink before I take you home?"

"No."

"How are things with Valerie?"

He shrugged. "I guess I'll find out in a hurry." He felt his pocket, craving a cigarette.

"Here."

He took the cigarette gratefully as they pulled up in front of the house. Valerie's car was gone. He got out of the car. "Thanks for the lift."

"Any time. See you later."

Rettick nodded.

"Good luck," the other deputy called as he closed the door.

Rettick walked slowly toward the house. He was going to need a whole lot more than luck. He unlocked the door and went inside. His eyes swept the living room, going beyond it to the kitchen. Everything was in the same perfect order it was always in. Sloppiness had never been one of Valerie's faults. In fact, there had been times when he and the kids would have cheered if she had left some kind of mess lying around.

He moved through the house to their bedroom and checked the closet. Her things were still there. That meant she would be coming home.

He went out to the bar and mixed a drink for himself. He found a box of Valerie's cigarettes in the refrigerator and took out a pack. He went to the living room and sat on the sofa, smoking and thinking.

He didn't hear the car, and he didn't hear Valerie come into the house. She walked into the living room, catching her breath quickly when she saw Mitch sitting there. He was bent forward, his elbows on his knees and his head bowed into his hands. Something about him gave her the distinct impression he was praying.

Valerie almost laughed aloud. Mitch? Praying? Never. Mitch Rettick would never talk to God. He was his own god, arrogant, mocking and needing no one but himself.

She opened her mouth to make some cutting remark, but something stopped her. She stood there watching him, not knowing what to do.

Rettick was still unaware that his wife had entered the house. He was aware only of that Presence that he had felt at the Cords' house during the night. He felt it drawing, drawing, drawing him slowly into Himself.

He felt the struggle mounting, peaking within his soul.

Run!

Run!

Run while there's still time! He'll absorb you, He'll control you, He'll annihilate you! Run before it's too late!

And suddenly he knew! He knew that the Presence was God, and he knew that he would always be restless, he would always have this craving, this hunger, this never-sated thirst in his soul until he let himself be drawn completely.

His breath became a sob in his throat.

"Mitch?"

He started violently.

"What is it?" Valerie asked, touching him. He was trembling! A shiver ran through her. She had never seen him this way.

He got up from the couch. "Valerie," he said urgently, "I have to find out about God. I have to know Him." The words came from him as if someone else had spoken them.

She was utterly, totally dumb-struck.

"You believed once," he said. "Surely there's something left of that."

"I don't know . . . It's been dead for so long."

"Come with me, Valerie," he pleaded. "Let's find Him together."

She saw the tears on his face and knew it was real. And from the deadness there came a tiny seed of hope and longing for what she had once experienced of God. She reached out and took his hands.

"You said once that Jesus Christ is God. What does He have to do with this?"

"We have to believe what the Bible says about Him. We have to believe that Christ is God's revelation of Himself to us. Through Christ we can know God, and we know Christ through the Bible."

"Then we'll get a Bible," he said. "I have to know Him." Rettick felt the very center of his being reach out to God. *Without You I am nothing. Take me. Take whatever it is You want of me. Take it all.*

He cupped his face in his hands and wept as a great feeling of release flooded his whole being, and the awful emptiness was filled.

Across town, Peggy Caldwell sat with her parents, holding her baby and rocking him gently in the big spindle-backed rocker that had belonged to her great grandmother.

"We were so worried," her mother said. "We hated to think of you being all cooped up in a little room by yourself for days on end. And this morning, after they got the streets plowed, we tried to drive to the ski resort to see if you were okay, and we couldn't begin to get through. If we had known there was an avalanche and that you went off the road. . . ."

"It's okay, Mother," she said. "Everything turned out fine. I'm really glad that I was snowbound with Jim and Jan Cord. She needed someone to be there with her during those awful hours when the men were searching for her kids."

"Poor little things! Do you think they'll pull through?"

"I don't know. I thought I'd call the hospital after awhile and find out. The only time I saw those kids was when the men brought them into the house half-dead, and yet I feel as if I know them—as if they're a part of me. I guess because I was there in the middle of all their parents' suffering."

"It must have been a nightmare for you," her mother said.

"Yes. All I could think about was the night Tom died." She looked down into her sleeping child's face and smiled. "You should have seen them. You should have seen how their faith grew. It was so beautiful."

Her parents looked at her sharply. Something was different. Something had changed in her.

She lifted her head and smiled at them. "I'm going to be okay now," she said simply.

And they saw the quiet peace on her face and knew that she had found her way back to God.

At the hospital, Jim and Jan Cord waited alone outside Emergency, their bodies drawn out with tension and fatigue, their minds devoid of thought or emotion. They didn't pray. They didn't speak. They didn't move. They simply waited, floating wearily on a sea of faith, knowing that whatever happened, God would never let them sink.

After a long time, the door opened and the doctor came out. His expression said nothing. They rose to meet him, bracing themselves for whatever had to come.

"They're going to make it," he said, "but some of their tissue has been badly damaged. Especially Brian's. Gangrene has already set in."

"Gangrene?" Jan whispered, horrified.

Cord supported her gently with his arm.

"Yes," the doctor said. "Most of the gangrene was not far advanced. Both children had some gangrene in their toes and fingers. This means that some of the soft body tissue has been permanently damaged. Fortunately, there's enough healthy tissue left underneath the gangrene so that it will be able to heal."

"What happens to the part that's been permanently damaged?" Cord asked.

"It will come off." He paused, giving them time to absorb what he had told them.

"You said most of the gangrene was not far advanced," Cord said. "That means some of it was?"

"I'm afraid so. Your son's feet were extremely frostbitten. I believe you said his boots were wet inside. It's too bad he didn't take them off. I was lucky to be able to save his feet. However, I had to amputate his toes. Too much deep tissue was destroyed. There was nothing I could do to save them. I'm sorry."

"At least they're alive," Cord said huskily. "Brian can learn to walk without his toes."

"Yes," the doctor said. "They're lucky to have lived through their ordeal. They were smart to find shelter."

"When can we see them?" Jan asked, blowing her nose and wiping her eyes. She had been crying quietly since the doctor had started talking.

"You may go in now if you'd like, although the

children have been heavily sedated. The frostbitten areas are red and swollen and blistered from the thawing, and they're very painful. The orderlies will be taking them to a room on the children's ward in a few minutes."

"We'd like to stay with them tonight," Janet said. "In case they wake up, we want to be there."

"It can be arranged, but I doubt that they'll awaken before morning. I would suggest that you go home and get some sleep. The children are in good hands."

Cord held out a hand to the doctor. "Thank you."

The doctor nodded politely and left. The orderlies wheeled the children into the hall. As they followed, Cord slipped his arm around Janet's waist and she leaned her head wearily against his shoulder. They went into the room and stood looking down at their two children.

"I keep asking why," Janet said finally. "Why did God allow this to happen? There doesn't seem to be any purpose."

"I know," Cord said. "Me too."

"Maybe we don't have the right to ask. Maybe we're supposed to trust God without understanding everything. I know God has a plan. I know He sees things that we don't see, and that He sees today in relation to all eternity. But it isn't always easy . . ."

"Yeah. I know," Cord said. "One thing's for sure though. He's changed us. We're not the same people we were three days ago."

He walked to the window and parted two slats in the venetian blinds. The sun was gone, but in the artificial glow of the lights in the parking lot outside, he could see that it was snowing softly, and in the space of several minutes or more, time was reversed and he relived those terrible hours when his children were lost. All the agony and despair and fear and guilt came upon him again, strangling his throat.

Then the memories passed, and suddenly he felt his soul reach upward to God, and joy and thanksgiving broke over him like a great, cleansing wave.

Thank You, oh thank You, he cried silently. His face, when he returned to his place of watch between the two beds, was wet with tears.